'Just what game are you playing, Paige?'

'Don't call me that! It's not my name.'

'Stop this! You know damn well who you are. And you know damn well that you had promised to marry me. Why did you do it? Don't you know what anguish you caused? To disappear without a word to anyone—and just a week before the wedding!'

'Please, I don't know you. I'm sorry, but I don't.'

'You must stop lying to me, Paige. If you don't I shall keep on hounding you, following you everywhere, giving you no peace, until you finally admit that you *are* Paige Chandos— my fiancée...'

Dear Reader

Welcome to  The **BIG Event!**

Everyone has special occasions in their life—times of celebration and excitement. Maybe it's a romantic event—an engagement or a wedding—or perhaps a wonderful family occasion, such as the birth of a baby. Or even a personal milestone—a thirtieth or fortieth birthday!

These are all important times in our lives and in **The Big Event!** you can see how different couples react to these events. Whatever the occasion, romance and drama are guaranteed!

We'll be featuring one book each month in 1998, bringing you terrific stories from some of your favourite authors. And, to make this mini-series extra special, we're highlighting authors in both **Mills & Boon® Presents** and **Mills & Boon Enchanted®**.

This month we're delighted to bring you Sally Wentworth's powerful, emotional romance RUNAWAY FIANCÉE.

Look out next month for BERESFORD'S BRIDE by popular **Enchanted**™ author Margaret Way.

Happy reading!

The Editors

RUNAWAY FIANCÉE

BY
SALLY WENTWORTH

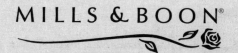

MILLS & BOON®

*First published in Great Britain 1998
Harlequin Mills & Boon Limited,
Eton House, 18-24 Paradise Road, Richmond, Surrey TW9 1SR*

© Sally Wentworth 1998

ISBN 0 263 80738 X

*Set in Times Roman 11 on 11½ pt.
01-9804-51506 C1*

*Printed and bound in Great Britain
by Mackays of Chatham PLC, Chatham*

CHAPTER ONE

JEAN-LOUIS had taken over the Eiffel Tower for the party. It was because he had become so famous—almost overnight, it seemed—that so many people had come to celebrate his engagement. Of course the painting was on display, and many of them had come just to see it. It was his finest work; critics all over France had raved about it. Suddenly he was fashionable and everyone wanted to meet him, to be painted by him, especially the women.

Basking in the adulation, and taking full advantage of it, Jean-Louis had invited the cream of Parisian society as well as his more artistic friends, all of whom were happily mingling here in the restaurant. And of course they were all intrigued that he was to marry his model; artists didn't usually bother to marry the women who posed for them, they merely kept them as their mistresses for a while before they moved on to the next face and body that fired their imagination.

The painting was hung in a prominent position, attracting a clamour of people round it, champagne glasses in their hands, their voices raised in knowledgeable praise. Many of them turned their heads and looked towards Angélique, comparing the living woman with the painted image. It had felt strange at first when people did this, when she'd heard them discussing her as if she were just an object, but she had got used to it now, was immune to their open stares and comments.

She overheard one woman, elegant, theatrical, say in a compelling voice, 'Of course, he was passionately in love with her when he painted it. Anyone can see that. The sexual awareness just screams at you.'

Eyes turned towards her again, some speculative, most knowing. This was Paris. Of course an artist would have an affair with his model. The only surprise would be if he didn't. Or, as now, if he offered marriage. With a flick of her long, corn-gold hair, Angélique turned her back on them and walked over to where Jean-Louis was the centre of a noisy, laughing group. People made way for her, and he immediately reached out and took her hand, carried it to his lips and kissed it in a flamboyant gesture. He was loving this, she could see. For too long he had hovered on the brink of being regarded as a great painter, but now he had arrived, now he could pick and choose his subjects, his pictures would command huge prices and he would, at last, achieve his ambition to be one of the *haute bohème*. All he had to do was consolidate his brilliant achievement. Already he had agreed to paint several commissions.

He put a possessive arm round her slim waist and drew her to his side. 'You are happy, *chérie*?'

'Of course. It's a wonderful party.' She spoke in fluent French, in which there was just the trace of an indefinable accent.

'Are you working on another painting of Mademoiselle Castet?' someone asked him.

The 'Mademoiselle' amused her; the guests were treating her with some respect because she was his fiancée, otherwise she would just have been 'the model'.

'But of course.' Jean-Louis opened his arms in an expansive gesture. 'How can I not paint her? She is so sensational. Her eyes—so beautiful. My palette cannot possibly do justice to them.'

People immediately began to reassure him, and it was true that he had painted her eyes with consummate skill, giving them their true brilliance, a vital glow, so strong that it seemed as if a light burned within her. It was Angélique's eyes that he had first noticed about her, their fire and their deep amber flecks against the intensely green pupils, and he had pursued her with single-minded determination until she had finally agreed to let him paint her. She had resisted for a long time, though, foreseeing this publicity and wanting no part of it. She had held out, too, against his sexual propositions, until Jean-Louis had become almost as frustrated about that as not being able to paint her. Almost, but not quite. With Jean-Louis his work would always come first. He had never said so, of course, but Angélique had no illusions about it.

A reporter with his camera came up, wanted to take her picture standing by the painting. It was far from being the first time it had happened but Jean-Louis was all enthusiasm. He went down the steps with her to where the picture was placed in the reception area of the restaurant, instructed the reporter on where to place her for the maximum effect, to get the light right. The man took a whole film of shots but by that time Jean-Louis had become bored and gone back to the upper floor. Angélique, though, stayed behind. Momentarily alone, she turned to look once more at her portrait.

Jean-Louis Lenée was an artist of his times; the painting was in the modern idiom but a recognisable likeness despite the richness of the colour and the symbolic background of rising hills and dipping valleys that, on closer inspection, turned out to be the voluptuous figures of women. Angélique's own, undeniably beautiful figure was tantalisingly hidden by a flowing white windswept gown that revealed parts of her and concealed others, leaving all to the imagination. But it was her eyes that held the viewer, mesmerising, hypnotic, teasing, alight with life and laughter.

She smiled a little. Earlier the woman had said that the picture had been painted with passion; that was true, but it had been the passion of frustration as much as desire. And Jean-Louis had been forced to use his own imagination about her figure because he had never been allowed to see her naked. Maybe that was why the picture had come across with such force, why the tantalising element was so strong. It was extremely erotic and yet at the same time possessed deliberate fragility, working on the viewer's imagination to create his or her own individual fantasy, to lose themselves in the picture.

A wide shaft of late-evening sunlight shone down on Angélique as she studied the painting, highlighting the profile of her tall, slim figure, turning the golden hair into a halo that melted into the light. She was wearing a white dress that reached down to her ankles, a gown not unlike the one she had worn in the painting—an idea of Jean-Louis's. The material was thin and with the light behind her became almost translucent, revealing the enticing outline of her shapely legs—legs so long they looked as if they started at her waist. She became a living painting, and far more lovely than the portrait in front of her.

A lift rose to the first floor, and the doors opened noisily. Chattering people came to the door, showed their invitations, walked over to exclaim at the picture and then went to look for Jean-Louis. A deep voice in good French but with an English accent said smoothly, 'I seem to have forgotten my invitation but...' The voice tailed off and Angélique could imagine money, a bribe, being handed over. Another gatecrasher; there must have been at least twenty of them there already. Moving away, Angélique ran lightly up the stairs and became lost in the crowd.

A lavish buffet, given as a present by the owner of the gallery where Jean-Louis was to have his next exhibition, was served to the guests. Wine and champagne flowed freely. The noise level grew higher, the atmosphere hot and overpowering. The room was circular, the walls windowed from floor to ceiling so that diners could look out past the metal girders of the structure of the Tower and see the landscape of Paris spread out below them. The sun had dropped low towards the horizon, outlining the surrounding buildings, black against the molten glow. Lights began to come on, piercing the dusk, romanticising the city. Angélique stood in the shadow of one of the metal struts where two windows joined, a drink in her hand, watching the throng. Soon the food and drink would run out and the more fashionable element would start to leave, to go on to other places. Only Jean-Louis's artist friends, the Bohemian element, would stay on to the bitter end, and then they would all go on to some club, perhaps Au Lapin Agile in Montmartre, and drink the rest of the night away. But not Jean-Louis; tonight he had other ideas in mind.

People came up to her, spoke, tried to draw her back into the party, but went away when she gave them no encouragement. But then a huge cake was wheeled into the centre of the room and Jean-Louis began to look round for her. 'Angélique. Angélique! Where are you?'

She reluctantly stepped forward, but then eager hands clasped hers, shouted that she was here, that she was coming. They pulled her towards him, the throng parting for her. She glimpsed faces, some that she knew—bearded artists, made-up models, suited men who ran art shops and galleries—but most were strange to her. But they were all smiling, laughing, pushing her towards Jean-Louis and the huge, vulgar cake designed like an artist's palette, towards the centre of the room where they would be the focus of all eyes.

Jean-Louis came to meet her, put his arm round her. He was a little taller than Angélique, about five feet ten, thin and wiry. His hair reached his collar but was clean and neat, and he had the lean face and thin lips that you saw often on French men. His clothes were good, bought with the large advance the gallery had given him, designed to impress potential clients and convince them that he would make a suitable house guest if he went to stay while he painted their portraits. His eyes gleamed down at her in excitement and anticipation; he was expecting a great deal from tonight—in more ways than one.

The art gallery owner, Jean-Louis's sponsor, stepped forward and made a speech, congratulating him on his success with the painting, prophesying many more successes in the future, promising his support. It was a long speech but they all listened good-naturedly and applauded loudly at every opportunity. Only at the end did the man remember this was also an engagement party and gallantly compliment Jean-Louis on the beauty of his fiancée and wish them both every happiness. Somebody put a knife in

Jean-Louis's hand, there was a clamour of shouts for him to make a speech, which he cheerfully did. His speech was a little more risqué, and there were some knowing remarks from his friends when he looked deep into Angélique's eyes. Then, the speech over, he raised the knife to plunge it into the cake.

'Just one moment!' The voice was sharp, authoritative, not to be ignored. With an English accent. Angélique recognised it as the voice of the gatecrasher she had heard earlier.

A man stepped forward from the crowd. About thirty-two or three, he was tall and very English, his shoulders in the immaculately cut dark suit broad, his straight figure strong and athletic. His face was cleanly handsome, with the hard, determined jaw that denoted self-confidence and willpower. And he looked completely out of place in this ornate, colourful gathering.

The crowd had fallen silent and there was an air of expectation as the man moved into the cleared space in front of Angélique and Jean-Louis. He was looking at Angélique, his eyes intent, but she returned his gaze with only natural curiosity. The man frowned, and then turned to Jean-Louis and said, 'I'm afraid this woman is an impostor.'

The artist gave an incredulous laugh. 'What are you talking about? Angélique is my fiancée. We are to be married.'

'In that case we have a problem.' The stranger again looked at Angélique. 'You see, she is already engaged to me.'

CHAPTER TWO

FOR a moment there was silence, followed by a buzz like that of a swarm of bees as everyone began to question their neighbour in hissing undertones, wanting more information but eager to hear what would happen next, not wanting to miss a word of a possible scandal.

It was Jean-Louis who spoke first. With a suspicious frown he said, 'Who are you? I don't know you.'

'My name is Milo Caine. I'm British.'

'Do you know him? Is what he says true?'

Jean-Louis had turned to Angélique, and the Englishman also had his eyes on her, his gaze intent, penetrating, as if he was trying to see into her soul.

She gave a small, amused laugh. 'Of course not. I've never seen him before in my life. He's probably a crank. And he's definitely a gatecrasher. Why don't you have him thrown out?' Taking hold of her fiancé's arm, she smiled up at him. 'Everyone's waiting; let's cut the cake.'

'Of course. Of course.' Turning his back on the man who called himself Milo Caine, he plunged the knife into the gaudy cake. The people nearby cheered and clapped, but with a disappointed air; they felt cheated of a scandal, of some excitement.

After cutting the first slice, he dipped his finger into the icing then playfully lifted it to Angélique's mouth. She laughed again and, taking hold of his finger, went to lick it off, her eyes on his, teasing, flirtatious.

'Maybe you ought to look at this.'

It was the Englishman again. Growing angry, Jean-Louis turned to gesture to the waiters to get rid of him, but then came to an abrupt stop as he saw the photograph held out towards him. It was an enlarged shot, in black and white, perhaps a studio portrait, showing two people, a man and a woman. The man had his arm round the woman's waist and was looking down at her with what appeared to be possessive pride, and the woman was looking towards the camera, smiling, but not with any great happiness; instead there seemed to be nervousness behind the smile. The man was Milo Caine—and the woman was unmistakably Angélique.

'And then there's this.' Before either of them could react Milo Caine showed them a newspaper cutting, again with a photograph. When Jean-Louis didn't take them, Caine let them drop and they fell on the cake. Then he started to take more photographs from his pocket, ordinary snapshots in colour this time, always of himself and Angélique. He kept dropping them onto the cake, covering its surface.

With a sudden snarl of anger Jean-Louis lifted the knife and stabbed it down hard into the black and white photograph, jabbing cleanly through it into the depth of the cake, and leaving the knife quivering there. 'What is this?' he demanded of Angélique.

'Maybe we could go somewhere more private and discuss it,' Caine said quickly, before she could answer.

Suddenly becoming very French, Jean-Louis threw his hands wide and said in a low, menacing voice, 'How dare you come here and say these things at such a time? Do you think I care that Angélique knew you

once? She is my fiancée now. You are nothing! Forgotten. It is me that she is to marry. Angélique is—'

'She is not.' Caine's voice, cold and sharp, cut
through his anger, momentarily silencing him. 'She is
not Angélique Castet. She is not even entirely French.
Her mother is English,' he said, his grey eyes watching her, 'and her real name is Paige Chandos.'

Both men had turned towards her, but Angélique
was unaware of their gaze. She was staring down at
the photographs, a stunned look on her face. Slowly
she reached out to pick one up, to look at it more
closely. It appeared to have been taken some time ago
because her face had a youthful, innocent look, and
must have been taken at a classy party because she
was wearing a lacy evening dress. Beside her, but not
touching her, stood Milo Caine in a dark evening suit.
He was smiling easily, completely relaxed, but again
she seemed tense.

Suddenly Angélique dropped the photo as if it were
red-hot. 'Jean-Louis!' She clung to him and, her voice
filling with distress, said, 'I don't understand. How
were those photos taken? I don't know this man.'

He looked at her, half puzzled, half disbelieving.
'But you must know him.'

She raised a strained face to his. 'I don't, I tell you.
It's some trick. Make him go away. Get rid of him.'

Jean-Louis turned, his chivalry aroused, and pre-
pared to do battle. But the Englishman drew himself
up, squaring his shoulders. He was taller, his shoulders broader, and there was a look in his eyes that
would have given anyone pause. Suddenly Jean-Louis
recollected that there were several reporters present,
as well as rich and influential people that he needed
in his career. It would hardly do for him to be involved in a brawl in such a public place. Especially

if there was any truth in Caine's claim—and even more especially if he lost the fight and was made to look a fool.

'Shall we go somewhere more private?' Caine suggested again. 'The restaurant manager's office, perhaps?'

He gestured with his arm and, agog with curiosity, those around them stood back to give them a corridor in which to walk. With an angry gesture, Jean-Louis took hold of Angélique's hand and began to stride along. Milo Caine followed them, first stopping to pick up all the photographs.

The manager began to protest but then saw the strained looks on their faces, gave a shrug, and left the three of them alone. He didn't shut the door properly. Caine gave a small smile, closed it and leaned against it for a moment.

'What is this?' Jean-Louis demanded angrily. 'What do you want?'

Caine straightened. 'I want Paige to admit that we were engaged.' He shoved his hands in his pockets, his face becoming set and grim as he looked at Angélique. His voice terse, menacing, he said, 'And I want an explanation. I want to know just why she disappeared. Why she took it into her head to walk out on her family and friends—and on me.' It was the first time he had betrayed any emotion, and even now he hadn't raised his voice, but Angélique was aware of deep, implacable rage that seethed beneath the cool hardness of his face.

'You're mistaken,' she said forcefully. 'I don't know you. You're mixing me up with someone else, someone who looks like me.'

Taking a step towards her, Caine said shortly,

'Anyone who has seen those photographs can be in no doubt that you are one and the same.'

'No, you're wrong! That girl is young, much younger than me.'

'They were taken some time ago, before you ran away. Why did you? Why did you go?'

He had come close to her, his face taut, his jaw thrust forward, and she could see that the hands in his pockets had closed into fists.

The menace in his eyes frightened her and she stepped back. 'I tell you, you're wrong. My name is Angélique Castet and I'm French. Ask Jean-Louis; he'll tell you.'

But her fiancé might just as well not have been in the room because Caine completely ignored him, instead reaching out to catch hold of her arm. 'Well, it will be easy to prove, one way or another.'

'What do you mean? How can you prove it?' Jean-Louis demanded.

'Paige Chandos had a distinctive scar, the result of a bicycling accident when she was a child. It's in the shape of a hollow circle about an inch across, on her left shoulder—like this…' With a sudden jerk he pulled her against him and held her as he tugged down the sleeve of her dress.

Angélique gave an outraged cry and Jean-Louis instinctively caught hold of Caine to pull him away from her, but then stopped as they both looked at her shoulder. It was Milo Caine who recovered first; he gave a harsh laugh. 'Well, well. How—convenient.' His scathing grey eyes came up to meet hers. 'A ladybird. A nice fat *round* ladybird. Now, I wonder when you had that tattoo done?'

It was Jean-Louis who answered. 'She has always had it. As long as I've known her.'

'And just how long is that?'

'Several months.'

'Paige Chandos disappeared just over a year ago.'

Snatching her arm free, Angélique pulled up her sleeve and said vehemently, 'I am not this woman you knew. You must be mad to think so. I keep telling you that I don't know you, that I've never met you before.' She swung petulantly away. 'Why don't you go away, leave us alone?'

'Do you deny that you're Paige Chandos?'

Angélique threw up her arms in exasperation. 'Haven't I already said so a dozen times? I've told you who I am.'

'In that case you won't mind having your finger-prints checked, then, will you?' Caine said smoothly.

'My fingerprints?' Angélique was taken aback.

'Yes. They can't be disguised—or covered up.'

Before she could speak there was a knock on the door and the owner of the art gallery came in. His voice impatient, he said, 'Jean-Louis, the American millionairess is looking for you. She's decided she wants her portrait painted, but only if you will do it immediately, before she goes back to the States.'

'Mon Dieu!' Jean-Louis smote his forehead in annoyance. 'Tonight of all nights we have to have this problem.' He swung round on Angélique. 'Sort this out. I don't care if you knew him in the past or not. Just settle this.'

He strode towards the door but Angélique grabbed his arm. 'Wait! You can't leave me here alone with him.'

He shook her off, impatient himself now. 'There are over two hundred people on the other side of the door; just scream if you need help.'

'No, I'm coming with you.'

She went to follow him but Caine took hold of her arm in a grip that was as strong as a vice, as strong as the embrace of a lover. 'I think not. You still have a lot of explaining to do.'

He pushed the door shut and then leaned against it before he let her go. Angélique rubbed her wrist, looking at him in wary defiance. 'What game is it you play?' she demanded.

Caine's eyebrows rose. 'Now that we're alone, I was going to ask you the same question. Just what game are you playing, Paige?'

'Don't call me that! It's not my name.'

He was suddenly angry again, and stepped towards her. 'Stop this! You know damn well who you are. And you know damn well that you had promised to marry me.' His voice harsh, he snarled, 'Why did you do it? Why?' Angélique lifted her hands to put them over her ears, to shut out his questions, but he caught her wrists and pulled them down. 'Don't you know what anguish you caused? To disappear without a word to anyone—and just a week before the wedding! We scoured the country looking for you. But all we found was your car, abandoned. I thought you were—'

'Stop it!' Angélique cried out. 'Don't shout at me. You're making my head hurt. My head always hurts when people shout at me.'

He let her go and she put her hands up to her head again, covering her temples, her eyes tightly closed, and leaned back against the wall. Grudgingly, after a few moments, Caine said, 'Are you all right? Do you want some water?'

'No. No, thank you. It will go if I'm quiet.'

He was watching her, gazing frowningly at her bent head. 'Do you often get headaches?'

'Not so much now. Not during the day, but sometimes at night—' She broke off, becoming aware that
she was confiding in this stranger.

But, '"Sometimes at night"?' he prompted. 'You
get them then?'

'It's nothing,' she said stiffly. 'Just bad dreams.'

He leaned forward, his face intent. 'What do you
dream about?'

She stared at him, then straightened up and gave a
scornful laugh. 'You ask me what I dream about? You
are mad, Englishman.'

'Am I? Perhaps.' He suddenly switched to English.
'I have your passport here; do you want to see it?'

Her eyes flicked to his, then away again. 'I don't
understand you.'

'Oh, but I think you do.' Taking a red-backed passport from his pocket, he opened it and showed her the
photograph inside. 'This was taken only a few weeks
before you disappeared. You needed it for the honeymoon we planned in America.'

He still spoke in English but she didn't react to it
until he thrust the passport at her. Slowly Angélique
took it and looked down at the photo. The girl it por-
trayed had made no attempt to smile, but seemed to
be looking at the camera with some reluctance.

'You'll notice that the description fits you exactly—even down to the scar on your shoulder.'

'I can't read English.'

'Rubbish! Damn you, Paige, stop this idiotic pretence.'

He went to catch hold of her but she dropped the
passport and backed away. 'No! Please! I don't know
you. I don't know you. I'm sorry, but I don't.' She
held her hands up to ward him off. '*Please*. Please,
leave me alone.'

He stopped, holding his anger under control at her obvious distress. His jaw tightening, Caine reverted to French as he said, 'I'm sorry, I didn't mean to frighten you. But you must stop lying to me, Paige.'

'I am not lying to you.'

Anger flashed in his grey eyes again, but with an effort he said, 'All right. So suppose you tell me just who you are.'

'I already have. You know who I am.'

'I know the name you've given me, yes. But I want you to tell me about your background. Where you were born. How old you are. About your family, your work. Everything.'

She frowned. 'No, why should I?'

'To convince me once and for all that I'm wrong.'

'Why should *I* have to convince *you*?' She flared up. 'It's you that is making all these stupid accusations.' Her mouth set obstinately. 'I won't do it. Why should I?'

'Because if you don't I shall keep on hounding you, following you everywhere, giving you no peace, until you finally admit that you *are* Paige Chandos.'

Caine had spoken evenly but there was a distinct threat in his tone. Angélique glared at him for a long moment, then shrugged. 'Oh, very well. I am twenty-three years old and I am from Normandy.'

'Oh, really? What part?'

'Lisieux.'

'I know it well. Whereabouts do you live?'

'I don't live there any more; it's where I was born.'

'But you must know it. Where did you live? Near the cathedral?'

He asked the question casually enough but was watching her so intently that she was suspicious of it. But Angélique shook her head. 'I don't know. We must have left there when I was very young. I don't remember it.'

'You haven't been back there?'

'No.'

'So who do you mean when you say "we"?'

She frowned. 'My family, I suppose.'

'You *suppose*? Don't you know?'

'Yes, of course.' She spoke irritably. 'My family. My parents.'

'And where are your parents now?'

A hunted look came into her extraordinary eyes. 'They are dead. Yes, they are dead.'

'And do you have any other family? Brothers or sisters? Aunts? Uncles?'

Slowly she shook her head. 'No, there is no one. I can't remem—' She broke off, her head rising. 'There is Jean-Louis. I am going to marry him.'

'As you say.' Caine was watching her, his brows drawn into a frown. 'Where did you go to school?'

A blank look came into her face. 'Here and there. I live in Paris now.'

His eyes narrowed. 'With Jean-Louis?'

'No. I have a room of my own,' she said with cool dignity.

His shoulders relaxed a little. 'Did you go to school here in Paris?'

She seemed to grasp at the suggestion. 'Yes. Yes, I went to school here.'

'Which school? Which district?'

'Different schools.' She began to move agitatedly about the room.

'Tell me their names.'

'I can't remember the names.' She turned on him angrily. 'Get out of the way; I'm going back to the party.'

But he didn't move from the door. 'You must remember the names of the schools you went to.'

'No, I don't!' Her voice rose, and Angélique put a hand up to her head again.

'All right. Tell me about your work, then. What do you do?'

Now there was no hesitation. 'I work at Le Martin Pêcheur.'

'What is that?'

'It's a big restaurant where you can eat and dance, on the Quai Victor Hugo.'

His face set. 'You are a dance hostess?'

Angélique looked surprised. 'No, I'm a waitress. That's where I met Jean-Louis. He came there to paint.'

'I see. How long have you worked there?'

She gave a small shrug. 'Ten—eleven months.'

'What did you do before that?'

Speaking with less confidence, she said, 'I was looking for work.'

'How long for?'

'I—I'm not sure. Several weeks. After…' Her voice faded.

'Yes? After? After what?'

'After I was ill,' Angélique said slowly, her hand to her head again.

His voice soft, not much above a whisper, Milo Caine said, 'You were ill?'

'Yes. There was—they said there was an accident.'

'Who said so?'

'The people at the hospital.'

'Don't you remember?'

'No. No, I don't remember.' She suddenly straightened up, said irritably, 'There, I've told you all you

wanted to know. Now leave me alone. You have
ruined the party for me.'

'There's just one thing more.' He took the newspaper clipping from his pocket. 'I'd like you to read
this.'

Reluctantly Angélique took it from him, glanced at
it, then immediately handed it back. 'It's in English.'

He made no comment, but took it back and said,
'Then I'll translate it for you.' But he didn't even
glance at the cutting as he went on, 'Basically it is a
report of our engagement. It states that our marriage
will set the seal on a business partnership between our
two families that has existed for over two centuries.
The company of Caine and Chandos has recently been
run by Milo Caine, the direct descendant of one of
the original founders.' He glanced at her to make sure
she knew he was referring to himself. Her expression
was one of wooden boredom, but he seemed satisfied
and went on, 'Half of the business, though, is still
owned by the Chandos family, but their shares have
passed through the female line since the death of
George Chandos in 1983. His daughter married a
Frenchman but the marriage was eventually dissolved
and the entire shares for the family's half of the company are now owned by his granddaughter, Miss
Paige Chandos.'

Folding the clipping, he looked at her expectantly,
but Angélique merely made a *moue* of disinterest.
'Why do you tell me this? It seems a strange way to
announce an engagement. Your English society pages
must be very boring.'

'It wasn't in the society pages, it was in the business supplement.'

She laughed and gave him a pitying look. 'So that
was what your engagement was—a business arrange-

ment. But that I can understand. They still have those kind of marriages among the wealthy classes here in France.' Her eyes disparaged him and her voice was taunting. 'No wonder you are eager to find your fiancée; how annoyed you must be not to have all those shares under your control, the entire power under your command.'

'Is that what you think?' he asked, watching her closely.

She gave an eloquent shrug. 'Why should you care what I think? I am nothing to you.'

'On the contrary. You mean a great deal to me.' His voice was warm, forceful.

With a small laugh, Angélique said, 'How can I when you have never seen me before?'

But Caine ignored her and went on, 'Is that why you ran away? Did you think that I didn't care about you, was only interested in the company? You couldn't be more wrong, Paige. I care about you very deeply.'

Slowly she raised her eyes to look into his, then gave a mocking smile. 'I always understood that Englishmen were cold fish—now I know why.'

His mouth thinned. 'I hardly think that the punishment you inflicted fits the crime, especially when the crime existed only in your imagination, Paige.'

Her eyes shadowed. 'Don't call me that. You're wasting your time. I am not the woman you're looking for. You've made a mistake. How many times do I have to tell you?'

Jean-Louis walked into the room. 'Are you still arguing?' he demanded exasperatedly.

'Do you read English, Monsieur Lenée?' Caine asked, and when he got a nod in reply handed him the cutting.

His eyes widening as he read it, Jean-Louis said, 'Are you saying that this woman is Angélique?'

'I'm sure of it.'

'If what he is saying is true then you could be rich, *chérie*. Is she rich, this—' he glanced at the clipping '—Paige Chandos?'

'Very.'

They both watched him as he stood silently, thinking it through, then Jean-Louis said, 'Is it really possible that you could be this woman, Angélique?'

'No,' she said positively.

'I've asked her about her background,' Caine interrupted, ignoring her denial, 'but she seems very confused. She said that she was in an accident and she doesn't seem to remember much that happened before that.'

'That's true,' Jean-Louis agreed at once. 'She has never told me anything about her past, her family. And I have never met anyone who knew her before I met her.' Going to Angélique, he said in a persuasive tone, 'If you are this woman, then it is only right that you should claim your inheritance, *chérie*.'

Her green eyes grew cold. 'What are you saying?'

He spread his hands. 'You may be right, he may have made a mistake, but—'

'He has,' she interrupted fiercely.

Jean-Louis frowned, then turned to Caine. 'Please, I wish to speak to my fiancée in private.'

For a moment the Englishman hesitated, but then nodded. 'Very well.'

When they were alone, Jean-Louis took her hand. 'I have agreed to paint the American woman's portrait immediately. Tomorrow I am to go to the château near Montpellier where she is to visit friends and do

the painting there. It will take me at least three weeks,
probably longer, and I cannot take you with me.'

'So?'

'Angélique, it could be that you are not this woman
the Englishman is looking for, so then, OK, you have
lost nothing. But you have always refused to talk
about your childhood, your past before you came to
Paris. I've often asked you but you've never told me
anything, except that you were in an accident. So
maybe you are this English girl.' He paused, then
said, 'Caine seems very sure that you are, but even if
you are not, what harm would it do to take this fortune
he's offering you?'

'I don't want money. I don't want to be rich. I just
want to be your wife, your model.'

'You will still be that, of course. But it's better to
be rich than poor. And think what we could do with
the money; we could pay off the loan from the gallery.
I would be free to exhibit my paintings wherever I
liked. I could paint what pictures I wanted all the time
instead of having to take commissions. And I
could—'

Her green eyes glacial, Angélique said acidly, 'And
you could wear Armani suits all the time, and go to
parties, and drink champagne all day long. You could
have a house in Tahiti and an apartment in New York.
You could travel and mix with all these beautiful, rich
people you so admire.'

'And what is wrong with that?' Jean-Louis demanded, incensed. 'A great talent should be nurtured.
You should be pleased that you could make me free
to do the work I want.'

'Pleased?' she said derisively. 'Pleased that you
could toss off a painting every now and again just so
that the women keep fawning over you?'

He laughed and pulled her to him. 'Ah, I see what it is, *chérie;* you are jealous. You think that if we were rich I would flirt with other women. But you know that there has never been anyone but you since the first moment I met you. It was love at first sight, was it not? I am your slave; I am the ground under your pretty feet.' He was kissing her neck, the corners of her mouth, her eyes. 'You know I adore you, that I would give my life for you. How could I even look at another woman when I am blinded by your beauty? Every moment away from you will be a lifetime. I hate this American woman for taking me away from you, but I have to do it. I can't afford not to. You know that.' He sighed against her lips. 'But if we had money of our own then I would never have to leave you.'

Angélique had her eyes closed, was listening to his insinuating compliments and comparing them with the Englishman's quiet 'I care about you very deeply'. Two such different men—one cold and aloof, holding his emotions under iron control, the other colourful, not afraid to speak or show his feelings. Or to use his charm to make her do what he wanted. Pushing herself away from him, she looked at Jean-Louis's earnest face and said, 'To be a great painter you need to work hard.'

'Have I not been working hard for the last ten years?' he exclaimed heatedly.

'Yes, and you've found fame at last. On your own. You don't need someone else's fortune. You can get everything you want on your own merit. Surely it's far more satisfying to do it that way?'

He grew angry. 'It would take me at least five years, maybe more, to get the artistic freedom I want. If you can get this woman's money I could have it

now, at once. Are you so selfish that you would deny
me that, deny the world my talent?'

'I was happy as we were,' she said bitterly.

'Having money will only make us happier.'

'No, it won't; money only brings trouble. I don't
want to do this, Jean-Louis.'

But he had seen a rosy vision of the future, and
having seen, wanted it, the freedom it promised shutting out everything else. 'If you love me,' he said
forcefully, 'you will go with Caine and try to get this
money for us.'

'Let me understand you. You want me to take this
money if it's offered to me, even though I know I'm
not the person he thinks I am?'

Jean-Louis gave an airy gesture. 'Why not? If he
is so eager to give away a fortune, why not take it?'

Staring at him, her eyes glacial, Angélique said,
'You are just like all the others, Jean-Louis. I thought
you were different, but you're not. I thought you had
integrity, to your art, at least, but you don't even have
that.'

He gave an impatient gesture. 'You're being stupid,
Angélique. It's because I want to devote my life to
my work that I need this money. Can't you see that?'

She didn't answer, just held his eyes with her own.
He looked away first, swinging round to go to the
door. Opening it, he called, 'Caine?' and the Englishman came back into the room.

'Yes?'

'We have come to a decision. Angélique has told
me that she can remember nothing before her accident, so maybe she is this woman you're looking for.'

Caine looked at them both for a moment, then said,
'I would need her to come back to England with me.'

'Very well, she will go.'

Looking directly at her, Caine said, '*Are* you willing to go?'

She hesitated for a moment, then nodded, her face set. 'Yes.'

'Having seen your old life, it may be that you will wish to return to it,' he said carefully.

Her eyes flashed fire. 'Be engaged to you, do you mean?'

Jean-Louis laughed. 'Just as soon as the matter is decided Angélique will come back to France to be with me.' And he put a possessive arm round her shoulders, then bent to nuzzle her neck in a gesture that was all confident defiance. Angélique stiffened a little but she didn't move away.

Caine's expression didn't change. He said, 'Very well—just so long as you are aware of the possibility. And, naturally, if she did decide to stay you would raise no objection; you would give Paige her freedom.'

With a cool smile Jean-Louis said, '*Paige* can do what she likes, but I assure you that Angélique will hurry back to me.'

It was a definite challenge, a glove being thrown down. Without any effort Caine accepted the challenge with a smooth, 'We'll see, won't we?' He turned to Angélique. 'Where do you live?'

She told him and he didn't bother to write it down. 'I'll collect you at ten tomorrow morning. Please be ready to leave for England.' Then, with a brief nod, he left the room.

Pulling her against him, Jean-Louis gave her an exuberant hug. 'We're going to be rich, *chérie*. And we still have tonight, just as we planned.'

Putting all her strength behind it, Angélique punched him in his midriff. He doubled up with a groan as she said, 'If you think I'm going to bed with you tonight after this, then you're crazy!' And she, too, marched out of the office.

A long, sleek car with British plates drew up outside her door at exactly ten the following morning, having to double-park in the narrow road. When Milo Caine rang the bell Angélique kept him waiting as long as possible, hoping the blue-capped dragon of a traffic warden who patrolled the area would catch him, but when he rang the bell for the third time she had to open the door.

He gave her a wry look but made no comment on her tardiness, merely saying, 'Are you ready?'

She nodded ungraciously.

'You have only the one case?'

'Yes. I don't intend to be away for long,' she told him coldly.

He was driving the car himself; she had half expected a chauffeur. Opening the front passenger door for her, he said, 'Would you like to take off your coat?'

'All right.' She shrugged out of the ankle-length coat and handed it to him. Under it she was wearing a sleeveless knitted top that hugged her breasts and a very short skirt. Her legs, long and tanned, were bare. His eyes ran over her and although his expression didn't change she could sense his disapproval. Giving him a provocative look, she deliberately crossed her legs, lifting the skirt even higher. Caine's mouth tightened for a moment but he still didn't speak, instead closing her door and going round to his own side of the car.

Angélique laughed. 'How stern you look, Englishman. Don't you like my legs?'

'You never used to wear clothes like that,' he commented evenly.

'It's not too late,' she pointed out mockingly. 'If you disapprove of me so much you can forget all these crazy ideas you have. Forget me. Go and look somewhere else for the woman who ditched you.'

A slight stiffening of Caine's jaw was the only sign that her jibe had gone home, and his voice was quite unemotional as he said, 'On the contrary, I'm quite sure you're the woman I want. And, now that I've found you, I don't intend to let you go.'

Huffily, she turned away and yawned.

'You're tired?'

She gave him a sideways glance. 'Very. I had to say goodbye to Jean-Louis last night. Remember? So, naturally, I am extremely exhausted.'

He probably didn't know it, but the tightening of his features gave away his inner anger, and she laughed again in ironical amusement.

The Paris traffic was heavy and required his entire concentration so they didn't speak again until the car was safely stowed on Le Shuttle and the train was carrying them at immense speed across France towards the Channel Tunnel and England. They sat in the passenger compartment in seats across from one another; the only other travellers were at the far end of the carriage, out of earshot.

'You said that you were involved in an accident,' he reminded Angélique. 'What kind of accident?'

Her eyes shadowed. 'I don't remember it. I only know what I was told.'

'And what was that?'

She hesitated, then said slowly, 'They told me I was on a bus. It was travelling along the Périphérique in a storm when a container truck jackknifed in front of it and they collided. Most of the passengers were rescued but then the bus caught fire and was destroyed. Two people were killed.' Her voice faltered a little on the last sentence, and then Angélique said, 'That's what they told me when I woke up at the hospital.'

'Were you badly hurt?'

'No. Just a bruised shoulder and a bad bump on the head.'

'How did they know your name?'

'There was a piece of paper in my pocket. It gave my name. It said ''Angélique Castet. Born Lisieux''. And it gave the date of my birth.'

'Nothing else?'

She shrugged. 'A few scribbled numbers and words that didn't mean anything to me.'

'Do you still have the paper?'

'Perhaps. Somewhere.'

'You didn't bring it with you?'

'No. Why should I?'

Leaning forward and looking at her intently, Caine said, 'Can you remember *anything* from before you had the accident?'

Her eyes grew troubled. 'Sometimes at night— when I dream, I see places that I feel I know, but in the morning...' She threw open her hands and made a blowing shape with her lips '...poof! They're gone.'

'Never people?'

Her mouth creased in amusement. 'No, Englishman,' she said in open mockery. 'I have never dreamt of you.'

He wasn't put out, instead smiling rather wryly. 'I left myself wide open to that one, didn't I?' She didn't return the smile, and after a moment he said, 'Look, we're going to see a lot of each other in the near future. I know you're angry with me and you don't want to do this, but couldn't we try to be civil to one another?'

'You are being civil to me.'

Again his lips twitched. 'All right, do you think that you could please be civil to me, then?'

'How?'

'You could start by calling me by my name instead of "Englishman",' he suggested.

'Very well, Monsieur Caine.'

'My name is Milo,' he reminded her.

Tilting her head, she considered the idea. 'I don't think I like it.'

'Nor do I, but I'm afraid I'm stuck with it, and it would upset my mother if I tried to change it.'

'You have a mother?'

'Most people do.'

Her face tightened. 'Do they?'

Reaching across, he took her hand. 'Sorry. Would you like me to tell you about your family? You do have one, you know, Paige.'

So he was convinced that she was his girlfriend, and seemed convinced, too, that she had lost her memory. With a sigh, she said, 'Are you always going to call me that?'

'It's your name.'

'And you want me to be civil to you and use yours?'

'Yes.'

She was suddenly angry. 'Why should I be civil to someone who has turned my life upside down, who ruined my engagement party, who has taken me away from my fiancé's side? You're a fool if you think—'

But he interrupted by saying, 'No, I'm giving you back the life you had. Filling in your past. You have the right to that. Even if you choose to reject it, you should at least have the right to choose.'

His words took her aback and she stared at him for a long moment before she realised that in his vehemence he had spoken in English.

Milo realised at the same moment and his eyes widened. 'You understood, didn't you? *Didn't you*?'

Paige didn't answer directly, but said, in perfect English, 'How did you know where to look for me?'

'It was the portrait. It was reproduced in an art magazine that I take. And it even gave the details of your engagement party.' Sitting back, his eyes on her face, he said, 'I would have known your eyes anywhere.'

CHAPTER THREE

'WHY did you lie to me?' Milo's face was grim.

Paige shrugged. 'Because I didn't want to go back with you, of course.'

'So you knew who you were all along. This amnesia thing is all a pretence, a ploy. My God, Paige, if you—'

'No!' She interrupted his growing anger fiercely. 'The woman you talk about doesn't exist for me. But I knew as soon as I saw the photographs you showed us last night that you were telling the truth, that you and I were—connected. I could hardly fail to recognise myself, could I?' Her face shadowed. 'But I was—afraid. The life I have is good. Why should I want to find out about a past that is wholly alien to me?' Her eyes met his. 'Why should I want to find out about you?' Looking away, she shrugged. 'So I pretended that I didn't speak or read English. I hoped you would think you'd made a mistake. That you'd go away again.'

'I'm not put off that easily.'

'No, but I wouldn't have come back with you if it hadn't been for Jean-Louis.'

'For his greed.'

She gave him an angry look. 'What would you know about needing money, Englishman? You've always had more than enough all your life.'

'How do you know that?' His eyes were watchful.

She laughed. 'You told me so yourself, when you quoted from that newspaper cutting. You said that my

35

family had owned half the company and yours the other half. You said that I was very rich, so presumably this company is successful. So, I repeat, what do you know about being poor and hungry? What do you know about having to prostitute your art to make a living as Jean-Louis has had to?'

His voice mild, Milo said, 'I didn't think that artists had to starve in garrets nowadays.'

'Don't change the subject.'

'All right. No, I've never been hungry—but neither would I push a woman into doing something she was against just to get money for myself.'

'No?' Paige's eyebrows rose in irony. 'But isn't that just what you are doing? Aren't you using me just as much as Jean-Louis is?'

His eyes grew guarded. 'In what way?'

'You say you were engaged to me. If we had married wouldn't you have got all the shares, all the company?'

'It wasn't a financial arrangement,' Milo replied steadily, holding her gaze. But he could see she didn't believe him, so he added, 'And, anyway, the question doesn't now arise, does it? You will be giving all the money to Jean-Louis.'

'And what if I do?' Paige demanded belligerently.

'It's your money to do with as you like,' he said with a shrug.

The train roared into the tunnel and they were silent for a moment, assimilating the change from natural light to that of fluorescence, from travelling on the surface to plunging deep beneath the sea. From openness to mystery, much as her own life had changed in the last twenty-four hours, Paige thought.

As if reading her mind, Milo said, 'Wouldn't you like me to tell you about your family?'

She sighed. 'No, but I can see you're determined to, so OK, go ahead.'

'As I told you last night, your mother is English and your father was French. You have dual English and French nationality and passports from both countries. Presumably you travelled on your French passport when you ran away. You were also brought up to be bilingual. Your father insisted on that. But when your parents split up your mother remarried and you were sent to live with your grandmother. She saw to it that you had a good education and—'

'Why?' Paige interrupted. 'Why didn't I live with my mother or my father?'

Milo paused for a second then said without emphasis, 'They had each formed new relationships. Your grandmother thought it would be best for you to have an uncomplicated life with her.'

'And my parents had nothing to say against the arrangement? Neither of them cared enough about me to have me live with them?'

Milo was listening for bitterness in her tone but heard only curiosity. 'It was—difficult. Your mother married an Argentinian and went to live there. Your father returned to his own country. They couldn't both have you. And your grandmother is a very strong personality; it's almost impossible to refuse her anything she sets her mind on.'

'But they could have, if they'd really wanted to, if they'd cared enough?'

'It wasn't that simple, Paige.'

She looked at him for a moment, then gave a slow smile. 'Life seldom is. Please go on.'

His grey eyes studied her face for a moment, but then Milo said, 'Your grandmother kept you with her at her home in Lancashire until you finished school,

then took you on a long tour of India and Asia that
lasted for nearly a year. When you came back to
England she brought you down to London to stay, and
that was where we began our own relationship.'

'We had never met before?' Paige asked in surprise.

'Yes, we'd met, many times, before your parents
split up. But not for some years and not as adult to
adult.'

Her eyes widened then grew amused. 'How old are
you?'

'I'm thirty-two.'

'And how old am I?'

'Twenty-one. Nearly twenty-two. Your birthday is
next month, on the seventeenth.'

'And when did this so passionate relationship begin?'

'You came to London about two years ago.'

With a mocking twist to her lips, Paige shook her
head at him. 'When I was only nineteen? Perhaps I
preferred older men—a father figure. Tell me, did I
fall head over heels in love with you?'

She was needling him deliberately but he didn't rise
to it, instead saying, 'Maybe one day you'll remember.'

Suddenly she was all French again, pouting her lips
and crossing her legs as she sat back in her seat. As
she did so her legs brushed against Milo's knees and
Paige glanced at him from under her lashes but he
didn't react. 'Somehow I don't think so,' she said
shortly. 'And my loving parents, are they still alive?'

'Your mother is. She still lives in Argentina.'

'And does she own part of the company? What did
you call it—Chandos and Caine?'

'Caine and Chandos,' he corrected her. 'No, the

shares she inherited were all transferred to you when she remarried. Your grandmother insisted on it.'

'She sounds a formidable old lady.'

'Yes, she is.' Milo's mouth twisted wryly. 'And not one to whom *I* would have entrusted the upbringing of a sensitive young girl.'

Paige frowned for a moment, then her eyebrows rose. 'You mean me? I was a sensitive young girl?' Her rich laugh rang out, making the other people in the carriage glance round. 'How quaint.' Her eyes taunted him. 'I'm no longer any of those things.'

'But you are still young.'

She gave a small smile. 'Oh, no; somehow I think that I've become very wise for my years.' Adding deliberately, 'And very experienced.' Seeing his mouth tighten, Paige leaned forward and said on a soft but compelling note, 'You would do well to forget that girl you talk about, forget her as I have done. Because she no longer exists and you can't bring her back.'

He met her gaze squarely. 'I know that. I shall have to get to know you all over again.'

'But you don't like what I am.' It was a positive statement.

'What makes you think that?'

She sat back, but kept her eyes on his face. 'You make your disapproval very obvious.'

'I'm sorry. I don't disapprove of you; I just find the change in you difficult to accept, that's all.'

'I expect people change when their circumstances change.'

With a sudden smile, Milo said, 'Now that is a very wise and experienced remark.'

She gazed at him for a moment, taken aback by the

smile, then flicked her eyes away. 'You didn't tell me what happened to my father,' she reminded him.

'I'm afraid he died. He had a heart attack some years ago.' Paige merely nodded and he said, 'It means nothing to you?'

She gave him an irritated look. 'What do you expect me to do—throw myself down and weep because someone I can't remember has died? Someone, from what you've told me, who more or less abandoned me? Of course it means nothing to me.'

Suddenly they were out of the tunnel and into daylight again. The train slowed for its journey through the Kent countryside and Paige looked out of the window for a few minutes before turning to Milo and saying, 'Is that it? Is that the sum total of this famous family you were going to tell me about?'

He nodded. 'That's about it.'

'So I've a mother, and presumably a stepfather, who live in Argentina. And a grandmother. Is that all?'

'I believe you have some relations on your father's side—cousins, that kind of thing—but no one close. And you have aunts and cousins in England on your grandmother's side of the family. I'm afraid neither of us comes from very productive lines.'

'When I marry Jean-Louis I intend to have a large family, six children at least,' she told him provocatively.

'Have you told *him* that?'

Smiling, she said, 'Jean-Louis is a very earthy person. He likes the sun and the open air, he loves light and colour. He's not like you.' Her eyes went over him disparagingly. 'You're an indoor person, without imagination, grey and colourless.'

To her immense surprise Milo laughed, the first

time she'd known him to do so. 'If you think that
then you, too, have got some relearning to do.'

Soon the train pulled into London and they got into
the car again. It was only then that Paige asked,
'Where are we going?'

'To your flat.'

'*My* flat? I have an apartment of my own?'

'Yes. In Chelsea.'

It turned out to be a garden flat in one of the quiet,
tree-lined streets that led down to the River Thames.
An old house of dark, weathered brick with a smartly
painted black front door. Very respectable, very gen-
teel. As she got out of the car Paige looked at the
street and the house with strong distaste. Taking a
small bunch of keys from his pocket, Milo unlocked
the door.

'You have a key to my flat?'

He glanced at her. 'You left your keys behind when
you—went away.'

He stood back to let her enter and Paige stepped
past him into a hallway. There were two front doors
facing her. The one on the left had the letter A and a
name-plate holding a card saying 'Major (Rtd.) and
Mrs C.D. Davieson'. The door on the right had the
letter B, but the name-plate was empty. After unlock-
ing the latter, Milo again stood back.

Aware that he was watching her, Paige pushed open
the door. There was an inner lobby that gave on to a
corridor lined with framed nineteenth-century prints.
The floor was carpeted and the air was warm. There
was no dust on the hall table that stood against the
wall, no smell of mustiness, only of beeswax polish.
No feeling that the place had been empty and ne-
glected for nearly a year. Slowly she walked to the
nearest door and pushed it open. It was a sitting-room,

quite large and ornate with an elaborate plasterwork ceiling, and luxuriously decorated in shades of cream and pale green, the carpet thick, the curtains opulently swathed. There was a wooden-framed reproduction three-piece suite, again in pale green, that hardly looked inviting; in fact it looked almost unused. There was a bookcase with leather-backed volumes—they didn't look interesting enough to be called books—which had probably been chosen for their decorative effect, and a couple of brass lamps with cream shades. A television set hidden away in a cabinet and a music stack concealed in its twin seemed to be the only concession to modern life.

Paige opened the doors of the cabinets, made a face, and walked out of the room to look at the rest of the place. There was a dining room with a pedestal table and six chairs that looked genuine antiques instead of reproduction, a kitchen with pseudo country fitted cupboards and, at the back of the house looking over the garden, a large bedroom. It had a four-poster bed, a dressing table and fitted wardrobes across the whole of one wall. She stood for a long moment looking round the room, then opened the door of one of the wardrobes and looked at the clothes. Pulling some out, Paige saw that they were mostly neat suits with straight, tailored skirts and jackets, and to wear with them there were long-sleeved silk blouses in pale colours. With an angry gesture she tossed them onto the bed and jerked open more doors. Every kind of clothes a girl would need, and all expensively made, but they were all drab, drab, drab!

Turning on Milo, she said vehemently, 'You have *got* to have made a mistake. No way could I ever have worn all these dull clothes!'

His lips twitched. 'I assure you, you did. And you looked extremely good in them.'

'I don't believe it. Even a nun wouldn't look good in these—' words failed her '—these uniforms!'

Milo laughed outright. 'I rather think you're working up to a good excuse to go shopping.'

Smiling in return, Paige said, 'I don't *need* an excuse to go shopping.'

There was a door in the far wall. Going over to it, she found that it led into a bathroom, the bath white, the walls pale green again.

'Is this a rented flat?' she asked in dissatisfaction.

'No, it belongs to you.'

'And did I choose the decor?'

'No, I believe your grandmother hired a firm of decorators to do it while you were still in India. She wanted it to be a surprise for you on your return.'

'I see.'

'If you don't like it you can always change it.'

The suggestion had been put in a mild voice but Paige didn't miss the implications. With a shrug, she said, 'What do I care? I shan't be staying here.'

Milo didn't argue, just said, 'I'll get your suitcase.'

Paige followed him into the corridor just as someone turned a key in the front door and came in. It was an elderly grey-haired woman, thin and very upright, wearing a pale blue woollen suit.

'Paige, my dear.' The woman stepped forward with her hands outstretched. 'How wonderful that you're back. I was so excited when Milo rang to tell me.'

Milo stood back but Paige caught his sleeve. 'Who is it? Is it my grandmother?'

A disappointed look came into his eyes. 'No. This is Mrs Davieson who lives in the flat upstairs.' He turned to the other woman. 'As I told you, Paige is suffering from loss of memory. I'm afraid she doesn't remember you.'

'How dreadful!' the woman exclaimed. 'But you mustn't worry about a thing. The Major and I will take care of you till your grandmother gets here. We're old friends of hers, you know; she and I knew each other as children out in India and then we were at school together.'

'Really?' Paige looked down at the outstretched hands. 'I see you have a key to the flat.'

'Oh, yes, we've been looking after the place for you.'

Paige frowned, not being able to imagine it. 'You've been doing the cleaning?'

'No, not personally, of course.' Mrs Davieson tittered with amusement at the idea. 'But making sure the cleaner and the gardener do their work properly, informing Milo here of any maintenance work that needed to be done, that sort of thing. Absolutely essential, of course, when the owner is away.'

Paige held out her hand. 'Well, I'm back now, so I'll take the key, please.'

But Mrs Davieson's hand closed over it firmly. 'I think I prefer to keep it. Neighbours should always have a key, you know, in case of emergency. And your grandmother likes us to keep an eye on you.'

'Does she?' Paige didn't push it but stepped past her and went into the sitting-room.

She heard the murmur of voices out in the hall, then the front door closed and Milo came into the room. He found her looking through the commercial phone book.

'Is this phone connected?' she asked abruptly.

'I imagine so; I've never had it cut off.'

'Good.' She found the number she wanted and

dialled it. 'Hello? You're the locksmith? I'd like the lock on my door changed, please. As soon as possible. It's urgent. The address?' She glanced at Milo. 'What's the address?'

'Twenty-two Bardell Street,' he answered slowly, his frowning eyes on her face.

Paige repeated the address and arranged for the locksmith to be there within the hour.

'Is that necessary?' he asked her when she put the phone down.

'You saw that woman; she wouldn't give me the key. Do you think I want her walking in here whenever she feels like it? Or her husband?'

'You could have thanked her for looking after the place for you.'

'Did you ask her to look after it?'

'Yes, I did.'

'Then you thank her,' she said ungraciously. 'Did you pay her?'

'A nominal sum,' he admitted.

'I thought so. That kind never do anything for nothing. Who else has a key and can walk in without bothering to knock?'

'Your grandmother has one. That's all, I think.'

'And you,' she reminded him.

'Not really.' He took the keys from his pocket and handed them to her. 'I was merely looking after them until you came back.'

'You didn't have your own key, even though we were engaged?'

'No.' His grey eyes looked into hers, challenging the mockery he expected.

She gave him reason to. 'So it wasn't a close enough relationship for you to come here whenever you chose, then?'

'I think that it's far too soon, and that you're in far too belligerent a mood, for us to discuss it.'

Her chin came up and it looked for a moment as if Paige was going to argue with him, but then she shrugged and said, 'Who else have you told that you've brought me back?'

'Your grandmother, of course. She's travelling down to London tomorrow and wants you to go back with her to Lancashire for a while.'

'To stay? For how long?'

'She didn't say how long. For as long as you like, I suppose.'

'I don't like. Who else?'

'Your solicitor. He will want to assure himself of your identity, of course, and then I expect you will have lots of papers to sign so that you can take over your inheritance. I've told him to be here at three.'

'He's coming here?'

'Yes.'

Paige laughed. 'How rich I must be, then, if the solicitor comes to me instead of me going to his office.'

'We thought it would be easier for you if he came here.' Milo glanced at his watch. 'Aren't you hungry? We haven't had lunch yet. There's a restaurant not far away that does very good seafood.'

'I'm not hungry. And anyway the locksmith is coming.'

'Ah, yes, the locksmith.'

He started to say something but Paige suddenly got to her feet and ran into the bedroom. 'Come with me,' she called.

Surprised, Milo followed her, but in the doorway found a pile of clothes thrust into his arms. 'What on earth…?'

'There must be a charity shop round here. Give them these. And these. And these.' She was pulling clothes out of the wardrobe, hangers and all, and heaping them onto the pile.

'Wait! Hey, wait.' Milo peered at her over the growing pile. 'Are you sure about this?'

'I couldn't be more sure. Hateful, dreary clothes. I wouldn't be seen dead in them. Come on, let's put them in your car.' Gleefully she picked up another pile and carried it out into the hall.

'This is crazy,' Milo said as they dumped the clothes in the back of the car. But he didn't seem at all angry, and looked, if anything, amused by it.

They made two more journeys before the clothes cupboards were empty, and Paige looked at them in satisfaction. 'Good. Now I'll unpack my case.'

She had just finished doing so when the locksmith arrived. Within ten minutes he'd changed the barrel on the front door and handed her two new keys. When he'd gone, Paige looked down at the two keys and glanced at Milo. 'One for me, and one for—' She paused deliberately. 'And one for Jean-Louis, of course.'

His left eyebrow rose and he said, 'Why do you enjoy taunting me so much, Paige?'

'Is that what you think I'm doing?'

'I know you are.'

Going over to the settee, she kicked off her shoes and put her feet up on it, showing a lot of leg. 'Why don't you come and sit here?' she invited.

She had expected him to hesitate but he came straight over, lifted her legs, then put them across his lap as he sat down beside her. 'Well?'

Paige's eyebrows rose in surprise but then her mouth curled in amusement as she recognised his ac-

tion for what it was: a deliberate counter-attack in this
war they were waging. 'Don't you ever resist a challenge?' she asked.

'Very seldom. Are you intending to challenge me
often?'

'If it amuses me.'

'Do you see this, then, as a game?'

'Of course. All life is a game—or should be.'

'Games don't have elements of cruelty. And I think
you're enjoying trying to be cruel to me.'

She didn't like that and went to move away but he
put his hand on her ankles, keeping her where she
was. Paige looked at the hand holding her and then
up at his face, but it was quite unemotional. After a
moment she said, 'How am I cruel to you?'

'You know full well.'

'No, I don't. Tell me.'

'By waving Jean-Louis in my face.'

'He's my fiancé.'

'And so, until a year ago, was I.'

Her beautiful eyes settled on his face. 'I can't believe that I was ever engaged to you,' she said in a
contemplative tone.

'You saw the press cutting.'

'Just because something is printed in the paper
doesn't make it any more believable. Was I in love
with you?'

'You would hardly have agreed to marry me if you
weren't.'

Paige jabbed him in the midriff with her toes.
'Don't beg the question.'

Milo turned his head to look down at her and she
noticed how level his brows were over the grey eyes.
It wasn't an open face; he didn't give his emotions

away, and he showed none now as he said, 'Why do you want to know?'

'Naturally I'm interested. If I was madly in love with you why can't I feel anything for you now?'

'Don't you?'

'No.'

'If you don't feel anything then why are you trying to hurt me?' he asked, coming neatly back to his own question.

Paige laughed and lifted her hands to clasp them behind her head, stretching the sweater over her firm, rounded breasts and revealing the fact that she wasn't wearing a bra. 'You took me away from my lover, so why shouldn't I be angry with you? And why are you so determined not to answer the question? Come on, tell me. Was I in love with you?'

Milo's eyes lifted from her sweater and came back to her face as he said lightly, 'I hardly dare answer you.'

'Why not?'

'Because I don't know whether or not you were madly in love with me, as you put it.'

Her eyes widened. 'Didn't I say I was?'

'No.'

She gave an incredulous laugh. 'Didn't you bother to ask?'

'One day I'll tell you about our relationship, but not now.'

'Why not now?'

'Because you're in the wrong mood, and I don't feel like having you deride something that was very precious to me.'

She studied the line of his strong square chin for a moment and read determined stubbornness there. 'I may never be in the right mood,' she pointed out.

But he said, 'Oh, yes, you will be,' on a note of certainty that she didn't like.

There was another question hanging in the air, a very loaded question. The atmosphere was heavy with the unspoken words. Looking into Milo's eyes, Paige saw the expectancy there, the slight tightening of his jaw as he waited for her to ask. She opened her mouth to say the words, then hesitated. She felt his hand tighten imperceptibly on her ankles and realised that this must be a moment of great tension for him. For a man who didn't show his feelings, he seemed in the grip of strong emotion now, and it disconcerted her. With a sudden movement, she swung her legs off his lap and stood up.

'I think I'll call Jean-Louis,' she announced. 'He will be worried about me, want to know that I've arrived safely.'

Milo, too, rose. 'Of course,' he agreed smoothly, all signs of tension gone. 'While you're doing that I'll take all the clothes to a charity shop. Have you any particular preference?'

She gave him a provocative look over her shoulder as she picked up the phone. 'Do you have one for fallen women?'

To her surprise he laughed. 'I can see I'm going to have trouble with you.'

Still holding the receiver, Paige watched him go, a look of astonished contemplation in her eyes.

That morning, before she'd left Paris, Jean-Louis had called her, full of contrition, full of endearments, carefully not mentioning the fortune she might inherit. She had allowed him to grovel for a while before forgiving him, and he had been overjoyed, but with just enough smugness in his voice for her to realise he'd known all along that she would. He had given her the telephone number of the château where he was to work, but she couldn't get through to him. The person who answered the phone, presumably a servant, said that he hadn't yet arrived. Paige left the telephone number of the Chelsea flat but no message. She was quite sure that Jean-Louis would soon return the call.

When Milo came back he had a big grin on his face. 'The women in the charity shop couldn't believe their eyes,' he told her. 'They were wildly excited when they saw the labels on the clothes but were afraid to show it because they thought that someone had died.'

'They were right,' Paige remarked. 'Paige Chandos died.'

'And was reborn as Angélique Castet.'

'That's right. Maybe I'll have my name changed officially,' she mused. 'That's if I'm definitely proved to be who you say I am, of course.'

Glancing out of the window, Milo said, 'Well, we'll soon know. Here's Charles Readman, the solicitor.'

He went to let him in. Charles Readman turned out to be a middle-aged man running to fat, a fact almost successfully hidden by the extremely good cut of his suit. A man from a firm that charged a lot for his services, Paige guessed. His gaze ran over Paige then he gave Milo a brief nod.

'I'm afraid Paige won't remember you,' Milo said before he introduced them, and added, 'I don't think you'll need me, so I'll be getting along to the office. Having been away for several days, the work tends to pile up.'

'You're leaving?' Paige asked, surprised at the sense of dismay the thought gave her.

Milo walked out into the hall and she followed him,

closing the sitting-room door behind her. 'You'll be OK,' he told her. 'You needn't be afraid of Readman.'

'He'll want to be sure who I am.'

'Yes, of course.'

'He might ask me questions I can't answer.'

'If you can't answer them, then you can't,' Milo said with a shrug. 'I'm sure that just looking at you has already confirmed your identity, but he might like to take an example of your fingerprints for comparison, just for the record.'

Her long-lashed eyes looked into his. 'To make absolutely sure.'

Milo nodded. 'Yes.'

'I see. Are you coming back?'

'Would you like me to?'

She gave an exasperated shrug. 'It's not a question of whether I'd like you to. You're the only person I know in London. I want to go out tonight, to eat, to have some fun.'

'All right. I'll come and pick you up at seven-thirty. Will you be OK till then?' He smiled. 'You can go shopping for a couple of hours.'

'I don't have any English money.'

'Tell Readman; he'll see to it.'

'Even though he hasn't yet made absolutely sure that I'm Paige Chandos?' she said on a sarcastic note.

But Milo merely said, 'He'll take care of you.'

She was with the solicitor for over an hour. As Milo had said, the man seemed in no doubt about her identity, telling her that he had known her since she was a child. He asked to see the scar on her shoulder and laughed when he saw the ladybird. 'You always were self-conscious about it,' he said. 'You would never wear an off-the-shoulder evening dress. But I'd never have expected you to go to these lengths to cover it up.'

'It isn't a real tattoo,' she admitted. 'You stick it on, like a transfer. When it wears off I stick another one on.' She gave him a mischievous look. 'But promise me you won't tell Milo. I've a feeling he hates it.'

He brought out an ink pad and carefully took her fingerprints, explaining, 'When you disappeared we called in the police to try and find you, and they took a set of fingerprints from here that they'll have on record. If they match they'll cross you off their missing persons file.' He gave her a look from under bushy eyebrows. 'It must have been an overwhelming relief for Milo when he found you, and an even bigger relief to know that you'd lost your memory.'

Paige met his eyes. 'Why?'

'When you disappeared without a word we all thought that you'd been kidnapped, perhaps killed. Everyone was frantic with worry, especially Milo and your grandmother. But then your car was found and—'

'Milo was frantic with worry?' Paige interrupted. 'How do you know?'

Readman gave her an astonished look. 'You were to be married. He's told you that, hasn't he?' And when Paige nodded he went on, 'When your fiancée just vanishes of course you're mad with worry. It stands to reason.'

'But he didn't tell you so?'

His face growing a little grim, the solicitor said, 'Milo isn't the kind of man to confide his feelings, but you only had to look at him to know what he was going through. He was in hell…'

'You said my car was found,' she cut in swiftly when it looked as if he would go on.

'Yes, in an airport car park. There were some things in it—jewellery, that kind of thing—which made it clear that you hadn't been robbed at least. The police concluded that you'd left of your own accord. Which, for Milo, I think only made it worse.'

After pressing her fingers on the sheet of paper, Paige went to wash her hands, and when she came back he got down to the financial side of things, giving her a credit card to use and a large sum in cash. 'This should cover you for now,' he told her. 'I'll see you again in a couple of days after I've spoken to the banks where you have your accounts.'

Paige smiled. 'After you've checked the prints?'

'It's purely a formality.'

He began to close his briefcase and she said, 'Tell me, have the bank accounts been frozen?'

'No.' He stood up. 'Your grandmother wanted to, but Milo persuaded her against it.'

'Why did she want to?'

Readman hesitated, then said reluctantly, 'She thought if you had no money you would be forced to come home.'

'I see,' Paige commented without expression. 'And has any money been drawn from the accounts?'

'Some on the morning of the day you disappeared. Not a very great amount. But since then nothing.'

He left then, and Paige took Milo's suggestion and went shopping. It was a long time since she'd indulged herself the way she did that afternoon; Paris was expensive and a waitress didn't earn very much, even with the generous tips that her smile brought her. But she had learnt to spend her money wisely and she did so now, raiding the cheaper shops that had more

colourful clothes as well as the up-market fashion
stores. In the lingerie department of one of the larger
stores an assistant exclaimed, 'Why, Miss Chandos!
But I thought you'd disappeared—' The woman broke
off in embarrassment and covered it by saying, 'How
nice to see you again.'

Paige made her purchase but as she left was aware
of several pairs of eyes following her and the whispered buzz of excited gossip. Ruefully she wondered
if her return would now be plastered across the head-
lines of the gossip columns. She tossed her head, not
caring.

Back at the flat she unpacked the gorgeous new
clothes, spending a while deciding which she would
wear that evening. Some of the new underwear, of
course, but it took her a while to make up her mind
whether to wear a very short and slinky red dress with
shoelace straps or a black number cut so low that to
move suddenly would put her in tantalising danger of
showing her nipples. Deciding that it would be more
amusing to have Milo on tenterhooks the whole time,
Paige eventually decided on the black. Pulling on a
new bathrobe she'd bought that afternoon, she went
into the bathroom to turn on the gold-plated taps of
the bath, but then heard the phone ringing. Turning
off the taps, she also automatically switched off the
light as she went out of the door.

It was Jean-Louis returning her call. 'Have they accepted that you're the heiress?'

'They took my fingerprints; they're being checked,'
she told him. 'What's the American woman like?'

'The same as all rich American widows,' he said
sweepingly. 'She will want me to make her look
twenty years younger.'

Paige laughed. 'All women want to look younger.'

They chatted for a time, the day gradually growing darker outside. Jean-Louis described the ideas he had for the portrait and she responded with interest, although France and her lover somehow seemed very far away.

Her mind still on Jean-Louis, Paige wandered back into her bedroom then, without turning on the light, remembered her bath and pushed open the door of the bathroom. The only window in here looked out onto the garden and she had pulled down the blind and closed the curtains earlier so that the room was in complete darkness. Or would have been except for a small round disk of light that reflected on the water in the bath. Standing in the darkness, Paige gazed at it for a moment, and as she did so it disappeared, only to return a moment or so later. Slowly she lifted her head to look at the ceiling. Because this was a ground-floor room, converted from what must have once been a lady's boudoir, the ceiling in here was also of ornate plasterwork, its swirls and scrolls an intricate pattern spreading out from the centre. The shaft of light came from the inner curve of one of the scrolls.

Carefully pulling the door to, Paige went back into the sitting-room and dialled the number that Milo had given her. When he answered, she said curtly, 'I want you to come here, at once.' He started to ask why, but she said forcefully, 'I need you. Just come, now!'

Paige spent the time waiting for Milo putting on jeans and a sweater. She was watching for him through the window, and as soon as she saw his car pull up she ran to the street door to meet him. Opening it before he could ring the bell, she put a finger to her lips, then reached forward and grabbed his hand, pulling him inside.

'What on earth—?'

Quickly she put her hand over his lips. 'Quiet!' she whispered fiercely. 'Wait here.'

Going back into the flat, Paige turned on the bathroom light, then began to run the taps again before running to rejoin Milo.

He was waiting for her, his face a picture of puzzlement and grim wariness. Taking the set of keys he'd given her from her pocket, Paige selected one but put it not into the lock of her own front door, but in that of the door marked 'A', and quietly turned it.

'What the hell are you doing?' Milo demanded in an astounded whisper.

'You'll see. Come on,' she hissed back, and began to carefully climb the stairs to the upper floor.

There was a corridor at the top, much like her own, that stretched the depth of the house. Through the nearest door they could hear the sound of a television set, turned up quite loud. Paige tiptoed past it, pulling Milo along with her, and went quickly down the corridor. At the end she paused for a moment, getting her bearings, then quietly turned the handle of a door on her left and pushed it open. It was furnished as a study with bookshelves and a large desk. There was nothing extraordinary about the room except that a man was kneeling on the floor with his back to them. He had taken up one of the floorboards and had his head down the cavity, peering down the hole he'd drilled in the ceiling above Paige's bathroom.

Glancing at Milo to see if he understood, she saw from the enraged shock on his face that he did. Striding over to where the man knelt, Milo put his foot on his neck. The kneeling figure jerked convulsively but was held down with such strength he was unable to get up. 'It's going to cost you far more than a penny to see this particular peepshow, Major,' Milo told him. Then he said to Paige, 'Go and get his wife.'

She hesitated, but then glanced at his face. Her eyes widened at the cold, contained fury she saw there. Without argument she went to fetch Mrs Davieson. She was sitting in an armchair, knitting, and gaped in astonishment when Paige first knocked then opened the door. Paige felt a surge of sympathy when she saw the knitting, but it quickly disappeared when the woman said indignantly, 'How dare you come in here without ringing the front doorbell?'

'You didn't ring the bell of my flat this afternoon,' Paige reminded her. She held up the bunch of keys. 'You said that neighbours should have each other's keys. Well, I have yours.'

Unmollified, Mrs Davieson said, 'That's for emergencies only. Quite different. What do you want?'

'Come with me, please. Milo wants to see you.'

She grumbled, 'I can't think what for,' but got up from her chair.

When Paige led her to her husband's study and she saw his behind poking up in the air, Mrs. Davieson went very white. But she wasn't shocked. There was indignation but no amazement on her face.

'She knew!' Paige exclaimed. 'She knew what this dirty old man was up to.'

His voice glacial, Milo said, 'You're out. I'll give you a week to find somewhere else to live. If you're not gone by then I shall make this public. And I certainly intend to inform Mrs Chandos, so don't look to her to help you. Do you understand?'

Silently Mrs Davieson nodded.

'Good.' Milo looked down at the struggling form of the Major and removed his foot. The man started to get up but Milo gave him a kick in the pants that sent him sprawling on his face in an undignified heap. Then he took Paige's arm and led her back downstairs.

He slammed the door of her flat, his face only now betraying his inner rage. 'The disgusting old lecher!' he said furiously, fists clenched. 'If he hadn't been so old I'd have taught him a lesson he wouldn't have forgotten in a hurry.'

'Somehow I don't think he'll forget it anyway,' Paige commented.

Something in her voice made Milo look at her and he saw with astonishment that she was grinning widely. 'You think it's funny?' he exclaimed.

Paige tried to control herself but began to giggle. 'It's just that—' her amusement grew '—I wondered what the Major looks like. All I've seen of him is his b-backside sticking up in the air!' And she doubled up with laughter.

He stared at her, then gave a reluctant grin. 'I'm glad you're not upset. You'd have a perfect right to be, especially as I brought you here. Damn the man,' he said feelingly.

With a shrug, she said, 'Don't worry about it. But I don't want to stay here.'

'No, of course not. You'd better pack your things again while I try to find a hotel to take you. Although it won't be easy at this time of year.'

Dragging her suitcase out again and thinking she was getting tired of doing so, Paige repacked her clothes together with all the new things. It didn't take her that long but when she went to rejoin Milo he was just putting down the phone. He gave her a rueful look. 'I'm afraid London is packed solid for a celebrity concert. I can't find a decent hotel with a vacant room.' His eyes met hers. 'I'm afraid there's no alternative—you'll have to come and stay with me.'

CHAPTER FOUR

'STAY with you? Where?'

'At my house.'

'OK.' She picked up her bag, ready to go.

Milo's eyebrows rose. 'Just "OK"? You aren't going to argue?'

'No, why should I?'

He gave a small laugh. 'I can't think of an earthly reason.'

Picking up her case, he led the way outside. Paige slammed the doors behind her and when she reached the pavement glanced up at the first-floor flat. A curtain twitched for a second as Mrs Davieson looked out and Paige lifted a hand to give a derisive wave. It wasn't returned.

When they were in the car she said, 'I hope his wife is giving the Major hell.' A thought occurred to her and she turned to Milo. 'What if they won't go? After all, it's their own place and—'

'It isn't theirs,' Milo cut in. 'You own the entire building.'

'I do?' She stared at him. 'Are you telling me I actually *chose* to live in that stuffy house?'

'No.' He glanced at her with a smile. 'As a matter of fact your grandmother bought it on your behalf. She was your trustee and decided to provide you with a home in London. She chose the place and installed the Daviesons in the upstairs flat.'

'So I had no say in it?'

'No, she did it as a surprise for you.'

'Well, I'm pleased about that. I was beginning to be afraid I'd actually liked living there.' She was silent for a moment, then said pensively, 'Is my grandmother a very dominating woman?'

His voice curt, Milo answered, 'You could say that.'

'Did she choose the clothes as well?'

'I should imagine she imposed her taste on you during the years you were with her.'

Paige smiled at the oblique reply. 'I guess I'll take that as a yes. Charles Readman didn't mention anything about the house being mine.'

'He probably hasn't got round to it yet. Didn't he say he'd see you again?'

'Yes, in a couple of days.'

'He'll probably go into things more fully then.'

She realised he meant when her fingerprints had been checked out. 'If the house is mine,' she said musingly, 'can I do anything I like with it?'

'Yes.'

'You said my grandmother is a trustee; does she have any say in it?'

'Not now that you're over twenty-one, no.'

'In that case I'd like to sell the house. I don't want to go back there.'

'Not even after the Daviesons have gone?'

'No. It's a boring house.'

Milo laughed. 'God knows what you'll think of mine, then.'

But his house turned out to be one of the few houses in London that still sat in the centre of its own garden. It was in Hampstead village on the edge of the heath, tucked away behind high walls and invisible from the street. Not a huge house, but a perfect Georgian villa to which some idiosyncratic owner had attached round towers, topped by domed turrets, at the two front corners. Inside, unlike the flat in Chelsea, it was full of things—ornaments, pictures, furniture—as if the past owners had delighted in buying *objets d'art* to adorn it. It felt friendly, lived-in, a home, not just a fashionable address.

Paige wandered round the downstairs rooms and came back to lean against a doorway leading into the hall where Milo waited. 'Do you live here alone?'

'Yes, I do. Is that a problem?'

She tilted her head to one side as she looked at him. 'Should it be?'

He gave a thin smile. 'No, but I can phone my housekeeper and ask her to come and stay if you wish.'

Straightening, she walked up to him. 'I don't wish. Which room am I in?'

'I'll take you up.'

Milo led the way up the wide wooden staircase to a room at the back of the house. It was a pretty room, with a draped half-tester bed, and again almost cluttered with things.

'This room was traditionally used by the eldest daughter of the family,' Milo told her. 'So it has lots of mirrors and cupboards.'

With a laugh, Paige said, 'You mean it should be OK to take all the clothes I bought today.'

'The bed will want making up. I'll get some sheets.'

They made it between them, Paige asking, 'Have you a sister? Did she sleep here?'

'No, I was an only child unfortunately. And the house is much too big for me, of course. I suppose it would be more practical to sell it and buy a service flat, but it's been in the family for so long that I hesitate to part with it.'

'Oh, but you mustn't sell it,' Paige said, horrified. 'It's a great house.'

'You like it? But it's about the same age as the one in Chelsea.'

'But that place is so staid, so unlived-in; this house looks fun.' The bed made, she said, 'I suppose I'd better start unpacking again. Are we still going out to dinner? Because I'm starving.'

'Of course. How long will it take you to get ready?'

'An hour?'

'Make it three-quarters—I'm starving too.'

Paige stuck to her decision to wear the black dress. The full-length triple mirror told her she looked good in it, the richness of the black silk a perfect foil for her long, straight hair. She was ready on time but deliberately kept Milo waiting as she transferred lipstick and comb to the little evening bag she'd bought to go with the dress and added some expensive French perfume to her neck and wrists. Finally satisfied, she picked up a wrap and went to join him.

She couldn't have contrived it better if she had arranged the scene herself. Milo was waiting for her in the hall and glanced up when he heard her step on the landing. He became still as he watched her pause for a moment at the top of the stairs and then come down them. The dress was ankle-length but it had interesting slits up the sides that gave enticing glimpses of her legs, and that low-cut top would have aroused any full-blooded male. Was he enticed? Was he aroused? Paige wondered as she watched for his reaction.

But Milo seemed in complete control of his emotions, merely saying, 'Let me help you with your wrap.'

Piqued, Paige said, 'Is that it? Don't you ever pay women any compliments?'

'Do you want me to pay you a compliment?'

'Yes. Preferably several.'

That made him grin. Reaching out, he ran the back of his hand down the length of her hair. 'Your hair is beautiful.'

'Is that the best you can do?' she asked in disgust.

'It's the colour of ripe barley in the sun.'

She digested this. 'That's a very—artistic comment.'

'More the sort of thing that Jean-Louis would say, I suppose.'

'Perhaps.' She looked into his eyes, sensing something deeper here but not understanding what it was. But the tiresome man's features were quite unreadable. With a pout she said, 'Oh, let's go. I'm hungry.'

He took her to Spaniards Inn, an old white-painted building not far away. The landlord greeted Milo by name and said, 'I expect you'd like your usual table, Mr Caine?' Adding, 'Nice to see you again, Miss Chandos.'

He led them to a table for two set in an alcove near the window.

'I hope you'll be warm enough here,' Milo murmured. 'I'd hate you to shiver in that dress—it could disrupt the whole room.'

'Oh, so you noticed.'

'Wasn't that the intention?'

Before she could reply a waiter came up to hand them menus, ask them what they would like to drink. Milo said, 'A gin and tonic and a small sherry, please.'

The waiter went to leave but Paige said, 'Hey, wait a minute. Who's having the sherry?'

His eyebrows rising, Milo said, 'It's what you always had. Sorry, would you like something else?'

'Definitely. A vodka and lime.'

Milo nodded to the waiter. 'So your taste in drinks has changed too, has it?'

'I wouldn't know. But I certainly don't drink sherry.' She grimaced in disgust. 'I don't even *know* anyone who drinks the stuff.'

'It's your grandmother's favourite tipple.'

'Really? Somehow I'm not looking forward to meeting her. What's she like?'

'She'll be here tomorrow, then you'll see for yourself.'

'That's really helpful.' She gave him a suspicious look. 'I think you're afraid of her.'

'Terrified,' Milo agreed, so calmly that she knew he wasn't.

Their drinks came and Paige looked at him contemplatively as she stirred hers. 'You know, there's one thing you haven't told me—and it's a very important thing.'

His face betrayed nothing but she saw his hand tighten on his glass and his shoulders stiffen as he said, 'Oh? What's that?'

She smiled inwardly; did he really think she was going to ask him if they'd had sex together here and now? Paige didn't answer for a moment, letting him sweat, then she said, 'You told my grandmother that you'd found me, but you didn't say anything about telling my mother.'

The hand relaxed. 'No. You and your mother haven't been close for quite some time. Not since you went to live with your grandmother. The old lady has old-fashioned, traditional views and she never forgave your mother for getting a divorce and marrying again, for splitting up the family.'

'Are you saying that my grandmother deliberately kept us apart?'

He hesitated, said, 'I don't know. You never talked about your mother.'

'You said she still lives in Argentina.'

'Yes. When you disappeared I thought you might have gone to her. But you hadn't, of course.'

'So she knows I disappeared. You wrote to tell her, or spoke on the phone?'

After a second's hesitation Milo said, 'No, I spoke to her personally. I flew out to see her.'

Her eyes widened. 'You went all the way to Argentina to look for me?'

'Yes. I wasn't quite sure whether your mother was telling me the truth or not. I thought she might be—protecting you.'

'Protecting me? Who from?' Her eyes met his. 'From you?'

His voice was firm, incisive as he said, 'Definitely not.'

She wondered about that, but said, 'From my grandmother, then?'

'Perhaps,' he admitted.

'So if I needed to be protected from her why wasn't it you I went to?' Paige asked, her eyes fixed on his face.

But he was looking down at his glass, twisting the stem between his long fingers. 'I'm not sure why you ran away, or even if you meant to stay away. You might have come back after a few days if you hadn't been in the bus smash and lost your memory.'

'Do you really think that?'

Lifting his head, Milo met her eyes, not trying to

hide. 'It would be nice to think so, but no, I don't believe that you intended to come back.'

'Why not?'

His lips twisted at her probing. 'It could be that you were unhappy with our engagement.'

'Do you have a reason for saying that?'

'You'd seemed very tense, as if you were under some kind of strain, during the last few weeks before you disappeared.'

'Did I tell you why?'

'No.' He shook his head in regret. 'I tried to get you to tell me what was wrong, but you wouldn't.'

'It doesn't sound as if we were very close,' Paige commented.

'We were—getting to know one another. You seemed highly-strung, nervous. And you were only young.'

'Are you saying that I'd changed my mind about marrying you?'

'Possibly.'

'And if I had would you have let me go, set me free?'

'That's an extreme way of putting it.'

'But would you?'

'I wouldn't have had any choice. But I would have fought tooth and nail to keep you,' he told her on a sudden surge of forcefulness.

Paige's eyes widened, but then she said sardonically, 'Why? Because you couldn't bear to lose something you wanted? Because you couldn't stand to be thwarted in your plans?'

His jaw tightened. 'It's true that I couldn't bear to lose you—because I want—*wanted* to marry you more than anything I've ever wanted in my life.' As he spoke, as if to emphasise the sincerity of his words, he reached out to where her hand lay on the table, but Paige quickly moved it away.

'Hey,' she remonstrated. 'I don't hold hands with men I only met yesterday.'

'I'm sorry,' he said tightly. 'For a moment I forgot.'

Perhaps it was fortunate that their food arrived then, because Paige was finding the conversation disturbing. After a few minutes in which they ate silently, she said, 'I think I'd like my mother's address.'

'Of course. Do you intend to write to her?'

'I might. I'm curious about her. Do I look like her?'

Milo smiled. 'I remember that her hair used to be the same colour as yours, but I think she helps it a little now.'

'She must be very much in love with her Argentinian.'

He looked startled. 'Because she colours her hair?'

'No, because she gave up her child, not to mention a fortune, to go and marry him.'

'How do you know she gave up a fortune?' he asked casually, but it was too casual and she knew he was trying to catch her out.

'Charles Readman told me. He said that when my mother remarried she signed over to me all the shares in the company that she'd inherited from her father. Did she do it willingly or was she forced into it by my grandmother—and your father? Was he alive then?'

'He was,' Milo said dryly, 'but he made sure he kept out of that particular affair.'

Paige looked amused. 'So was it an affair? Was she hopelessly in love?'

'Presumably she was in love. Whether it was hopelessly or not, I don't know.'

Paige smiled openly. 'Oh, I think that to have an affair one should always be hopelessly in love.' She lifted her glass and looked at him over its rim as she sipped the wine. 'Passionately, fervently in love. Anything less would be very boring, don't you think?'

Milo knew that she was baiting him again, but he said smoothly, 'Of course.' Adding, 'You have a habit of doing that.'

'Doing what?'

'Looking at me over your glass. Is it supposed to be very sexy or something?'

She looked at him for a moment then gave a peal of laughter. 'What an *English* remark! I should have introduced you to some girlfriends of mine in Paris. I can see you need educating where women are concerned.'

Milo's eyebrows rose. 'Good heavens—you have lost your memory!'

A remark which left Paige completely lost for words.

After that they both decided it was best to keep the conversation on a social level. Paige asked him about the company of which she was now a half-shareholder, and he told her of its beginning from a smallish enterprise that had gradually and judiciously been increased over the years until it was now a major name in the commercial world.

'Do you run it?' she asked.

'I'm the managing director,' he admitted. 'But obviously there is a large staff to run it.'

'I'd like to go there one day.'

He looked surprised. 'Of course.'

'Didn't I ever want to before?'

'No. Your grandfather used to take you sometimes when you were a little girl. He'd sit you on his knee

during board meetings. I don't think the other directors approved but he used to say that the company
would be half yours one day and he wanted you to
learn everything about it. But once he died your
grandmother put a stop to that.' He gave a nostalgic
smile. 'That's mostly where I used to see you. My
father used to take me along during the school holi-
days, to get to know the atmosphere. He wanted the
place to be in my blood, I suppose.'

'And it worked,' Paige said lightly. 'The company
is obviously the most important thing in your life.'

His grey eyes growing a little cold, he said, 'Why
do you say that?'

She shrugged. 'What else do you have to concentrate on? Unless, of course, you've met someone else,
someone you've fallen for.'

He gave her an odd look. 'No. I haven't met anyone
else.' Milo changed the subject then, asking her how
she'd got on in Paris when she'd lost her memory.
'Presumably you were without money or papers?'

'Yes, but it wasn't difficult. There was a charity
which helped. But I soon found a job at the dance
hall, and one of the girls there had a spare room in
her apartment that I was able to rent.'

'I wonder who the real Angelique Castet, is.'

She looked intrigued. 'I hadn't thought of that.
Maybe one day I'll try and find out.' Paige laughed,
her eyes full of amusement. 'But perhaps not; she may
not approve of me borrowing her name.'

'On the contrary, she ought to be very flattered,'
Milo remarked, his eyes smiling.

It was a nice compliment, subtle and understated,
but a definite compliment. Paige studied him as he
turned to speak to the landlord who had come up to
ask if the meal was OK. Milo chatted to him easily,

as if they were old acquaintances, which they probably were as he lived so close. There was nothing patronising about Milo; he was spoken to as an equal, not just a valued customer, as they discussed the progress of the British cricket team on their tour of the West Indies. And the landlord obviously liked him as a person; he spent far longer at their table than at any other.

But the fact that Milo got on with a restaurateur didn't necessarily mean that he had made an ideal fiancé, Paige reminded herself. He had told her a little of their relationship but not much. She realised that there was still a lot to learn, especially about why she had run away. On the surface it would appear to have been a very unnatural and stupid thing to do. Because—on the surface—Milo would seem to be an ideal person to marry, to be in love with. He was tall, good-looking, civilised, wealthy. What more could a girl want? A whole lot more, she answered herself at once. Excitement for a start. And the knowledge that he could be overpowered by love, by sexual need, lust. By whatever name you called it so long as it consumed him, carried him along on a great tide of passion that was beyond his control.

But somehow Paige couldn't imagine that calm, self-possessed face, that lean, athletic body ever being so out of control that he would do anything for love. When they had first been alone, back in the manager's office at the Eiffel Tower, when he hadn't known she'd lost her memory, he had shown anger then, admittedly. But when he had talked of loving her he definitely hadn't shown it. Maybe it was true, maybe he had loved her, but who wanted to be loved by a man who was incapable of showing his emotions? Give her Jean-Louis any day.

When they came out of the restaurant, it was a clear but crisp night. Somewhere on the heath a night bird was singing its heart out, the sound fluting through the air, and under the hedge a pair of rabbits bolted into a hole. Paige smiled. 'It must be spring.' She turned to Milo. 'How far is it to your house?'

'About a mile.'

'Let's walk.'

'All right.' He dropped his car keys back into his pocket.

'Don't you mind leaving your car?'

He shrugged. 'It's as safe there as anywhere.'

They began to stroll along the pavement, Paige swinging her bag by its strap. 'Tell me about yourself,' she invited. 'What do you do in your spare time?'

'Why do you want to know?'

There was surprise in her voice as Paige said, 'Don't you want me to be interested in you?'

'Are you?'

'You tell me I was engaged to you, so naturally I'm curious.'

'I see. So it's just curiosity. OK, let's see if I can satisfy it, then.' His voice was terse, distant. 'I'm afraid I don't seem to have had much spare time during the past year, but when I have I enjoy reading, sport, music, but most of all I like collecting pictures.'

The reference to the past year wasn't lost on Paige but she chose to ignore it, saying, 'Of course—art. That's how you came to see a photograph of Jean-Louis's portrait of me, which led you to our engagement party.' And added casually, to tease him, 'It was the portrait you saw, wasn't it? Not one of the nude studies?'

Milo was silent for just a moment too long before he said, 'No, it was the portrait.'

'Do you paint yourself?'

'No, I leave that to those with talent.'

'Do you think Jean-Louis has talent?'

'Yes, but he needs to develop it.'

'Perhaps you should buy my portrait from him,' Paige suggested flippantly. 'After all, it is of your ex-fiancée.'

'And of his.'

'Oh, no, I'm still engaged to *him*.'

It was difficult to read Milo's expression in the darkness but Paige thought he smiled slightly before saying, 'Do you think he would sell the painting?'

Paige laughed. 'I can see you're trying to trap me. Of course he wouldn't part with it. Although he can, of course, paint me any time he likes. However he likes,' she added provocatively.

'As you pointed out,' was all Milo would say, but there was a touch of irony in his voice.

They reached a street corner, Paige slightly ahead, and she turned to the left. Following, Milo said, 'You seem to know the way.'

Swinging round, she said, 'Isn't this the way we came?'

He nodded, but she had noted the touch of steel in his voice and his face. He was still trying to catch her out, then. He still wasn't absolutely sure that she'd lost her memory. For a second Paige felt a frisson of something close to fear; she could only guess at his anger if he ever became convinced that she was deceiving him, playing some deep game. Any man would be angry at being deceived in such circumstances, she knew that, but somehow she thought that with Milo it would go deeper. But whether it would be through hurt pride or through some more basic and infinitely more important emotion she couldn't tell. But it didn't matter; he would soon stop being suspicious of her, stop setting little traps into which he hoped she might fall. Or perhaps he didn't want her to fall into them; perhaps he preferred her to have lost her memory, so that he could tell her his own version of her flight to France.

The wind had risen a little and caught her cape, blowing it off one shoulder. Paige exclaimed and made a grab for it, then laughed as it was lifted into the air and threatened to blow away. But Milo was quicker and caught it easily. He stepped to put it back round her shoulders, but the wind had caught her hair and spun it into a golden frame for her head. She was laughing, putting up a hand to shield her face, the skin of her arms and bare shoulders like silk in the moonlight. For a long moment Milo just stood and watched her—she was so full of vitality, so lovely—but then he blinked and came to shelter her from the wind as he put the cape back round her. As he did so they were very close, their bodies almost touching. Paige could smell his aftershave, was aware of the breadth of his shoulders, his strong masculinity. Lifting her head, she looked into his face, but it was too dark to tell if there was need in his eyes, whether or not he wanted her. She didn't move away, let him step back first, then she gave a small laugh, as if that was what she'd expected, and began to walk on again.

They reached the house and Milo unlocked the door for her. It wasn't very late, not yet eleven o'clock. Instead of going upstairs to her room, Paige went into the sitting-room. 'Can I have a drink?'

'Of course. You're not tired?'

'No.' She sat down on the settee, crossed her long

legs so that the split in her skirt fell open, revealing them. 'Did you think I was?'

'Before—you often used to be tired and wanted to be taken straight home—or at least you said you were.'

'Maybe I was tired of you.'

She saw him flinch a little at that, but he said, 'Perhaps you're right.' He poured then handed her a drink and went to sit in an armchair by the side of the unlit fire. 'You've changed a great deal since you've been away.'

'You mean I look different?'

'Not that so much, but in your mental attitude. You were very shy, very reserved before. Now you're much more sure of yourself. You would never have—' he paused to choose the word carefully '—sparred with me before.'

'How do you mean?'

'Oh, I think you know.'

She pouted. 'No, tell me.'

'You constantly try to provoke me. And please don't try to tell me that it's because I took you away from Jean-Louis. I think it goes much deeper than that.'

'How could it?'

'Perhaps, in your subconscious, you need to get some reaction from me.'

Paige looked at him for a moment, then said, 'Why did I run away from you? There must have been a reason.' He didn't answer so she put her drink down and got angrily to her feet. 'You've got to tell me, don't you realise that? How can I ever trust you if I don't know what it was that drove me away? Did we have a fight? Is that it? Did I want to break off the engagement for some reason?'

Milo had been watching her, his hands gripping the arms of his chair, but now he too rose. 'I don't know why you ran away. Do you think I didn't spend every waking moment racking my brains to discover why? If you remember, I asked you yesterday why you'd gone. You didn't leave a note, nothing. It was the most cruel thing to do.'

'And was I a cruel person?'

That brought him up short. 'No. No, I would have said you were completely the opposite. It was completely uncharacteristic of you. But during those last weeks you'd seemed different, very withdrawn. I'd put it down to pre-wedding nerves, but obviously it must have been something much more serious than that.'

'When was the last time we met? Tell me about that.'

He didn't have to think about it. 'It was the day before you disappeared. We'd gone to the church for a rehearsal of the wedding. Your grandmother had arranged the ceremony and she insisted on a run-through. It should have been a happy time, but you hardly spoke to anyone.' He paused, then said, 'I remember you had a handkerchief in your hand, some silly little piece of linen and lace. You stood there and gradually tore it to pieces. I saw that you were under a great deal of stress and was just glad that in a week it would all be over, that I would be able to take you away and we could relax.'

'Are you sure you knew of nothing that could have made me feel unhappy?'

'Quite sure.' He paused. 'No, that isn't absolutely true.' Paige's eyes came swiftly up to his face, but he didn't look unduly perturbed as he said slowly, 'Your grandmother had always wanted us to marry. She has a great sense of history, and it was her dearest wish to unite the two families at last. In the past a Chandos had once married a Caine but the wife died in childbirth so there was no heir to carry both names into the future. When she brought you to London I'm afraid she made it plain to both of us that it was what she wished for.'

'She just came out and said it?'

'Not in so many words, no. But she has ways of making her wishes felt, probably to you more than me. I was afraid that she'd coerced you into something you weren't quite ready for.'

She gave him an odd look. 'But you still fell in with her wishes. You went ahead with the engagement, the wedding.'

'Yes, I thought it important to get you away from her—influence.'

Her voice becoming brittle, Paige said, 'From hers to yours. And of course it suited you to marry me. How convenient that you should fall for me.'

'Once I'd seen you, all grown up and so lovely, I had no choice in the matter,' Milo told her simply.

She looked at him for a moment, then laughed. 'You "had no choice in the matter".' She mimicked his words. 'What a lover-like expression! No wonder I didn't want to marry you.' She saw his face whiten, become tense. He was sensitive here, she realised, and she had no hesitation in taking advantage of his apparent weakness. 'Tell me.' Her voice grew contemptuous. 'Is that the way you behave to all your women? Do you keep the whole thing brisk and businesslike?'

Milo's hands balled into fists held tightly against his sides as he said, 'There are no other women in my life.'

'No? Am I supposed to be flattered by that?' Her

voice grew derisively sarcastic. 'Have you really been pining for your lost little teenager? The innocent dupe who was to unite the company shares? And if I hadn't gone away would you have gone on being so polite, so restrained once we were married? Presumably you show some feeling when you take a woman to bed. Or is sex just a matter of impersonal convenience, too?'

Milo strode over and took hold of her wrist, his grip like a steel manacle. 'It was never impersonal between us.'

'What?' she said jeeringly. 'A cold fish like you actually daring to show some emotion? I don't believe it. You're far too controlled to ever—'

But Milo had taken hold of her other arm, and, his face taut, said, 'What are you trying to do with your taunts, Paige? To provoke me beyond endurance? Until I can't stand the hurt any more?'

'Hurt? I don't believe you feel any real pain. The only part of you that got hurt was your insufferable pride!'

His face very tense, his eyes blazing, Milo said, 'Damn you, you just went too far!' Jerking her towards him, he said, 'Is this what you want? Is it?' And he took her roughly into his arms and brought his mouth down, hard and bruising, against hers.

CHAPTER FIVE

PAIGE had deliberately provoked Milo into this, but now she found it almost more than she could handle, more than she could bear. His kiss, born of emotions too long restrained, too long feeding on fear and pain, suddenly erupted into almost savage hunger. His lips seemed to burn into hers, to demand expiation for all the long months of searching. It was compulsive, selfish, and spoke of desperate need.

She gasped against his mouth, but Milo took it for a sign of rejection because his hold on her tightened until she was powerless to move. His mouth ravaged hers, and if she had ever thought him empty of emotion the idea was not only killed stone dead, but was completely annihilated. There was no gentleness here. She was his prisoner, the captive of his arms and his lips. It was as if, having found her, he never intended to let her go again. It never occurred to Paige to struggle; she knew it would be a waste of time. But she didn't return the kiss, just accepted it, letting him do what he wanted.

By the time he let her go her head had begun to whirl, but she managed to lift angry, defiant eyes to his. Almost as a reflex action her hand came up to hit him, but Milo saw it coming a mile off and caught her wrist. For a moment they stared into each other's eyes, both smouldering with inner emotions that were too fierce for words. Then Milo simply pulled her against him and kissed her again.

This time, afraid of being sucked again into the

80

maelstrom, she tried to struggle. But, where there had been only hunger for revenge in his lips, now there was also sensuality, a different kind of hunger. It evoked a bewildering response in her—a deep yearning for something lost but only vaguely remembered, like half-forgotten dreams, something held deep in her soul. A secret to which only his kiss held the key. As soon as she felt it, Paige panicked. Putting her arms against his chest, she somehow managed to push him away. Again they stared at one another. Milo's breath was heavy, ragged, and a lock of dark hair had fallen onto his forehead. He looked a different man from the austere, contained person who had brought her home from France only that morning.

'How dare you?' she said fiercely. 'Do you think I want your disgusting kisses? Do you think I want you touching me?'

'You didn't always find them so obnoxious,' he told her curtly. 'In fact, you used to quite enjoy them.'

Recovering a little, realising that she, too, was betraying emotion, Paige laughed. 'There is a great difference between an innocent nineteen-year-old and a woman. What I might have found enjoyable then I find only—' she tried to think of a word that would devastate him '—pitiable now,' she said on a vicious note.

His jaw hardened. 'So you're a woman now, are you?' Impatiently he pushed the lock of hair off his face.

'Of course. And Frenchmen are everything they're reputed to be. They're not barbaric like you. They have finesse, subtlety, they know how to excite a woman. They don't think that if they just hold you tight enough and kiss you hard enough then you'll be overcome with their macho image and fall into bed with them. Frenchmen know how to woo a woman, how to lift her to the heights of pleasure,' she taunted.

His face grim, Milo said, 'And are you speaking in general terms or from personal experience?'

'From personal experience, of course.'

'Frenchmen? In the plural?'

'Yes. French *men*.'

His hands had again balled into fists. 'I see.'

'No, you don't,' she said angrily. 'You know nothing about me. So don't stand there looking like some outraged Victorian. I'm my own person and I shall do exactly as I like.'

Milo stood, watching the defiant way she faced up to him, her extraordinary eyes flashing fire, her chin up and shoulders stiffened, ready to fight him. To her surprise his face relaxed a little, and he said unexpectedly, 'I hate to talk in clichés, but you look amazingly beautiful when you're angry.'

She was taken aback, but recovered quickly. 'Don't think you can get out of this by flattery. You had no right to kiss me.'

'On the contrary, I have every right.'

His voice had grown silky, making her look at him with some misgivings. She sensed a hidden meaning, but wasn't yet ready to pursue it, so said, 'You may think you have because we were once engaged, but you forget that to me you're a stranger—and I'm not in the habit of letting strangers kiss me.'

'Really?' It was Milo's turn to mock. 'But what about all those Frenchmen you've just been goading me with?'

Without hesitation Paige took up the challenge and flung his mockery back at him. 'Oh, but they weren't *strangers*.'

If the dart went home Milo didn't show it. Dryly

he said, 'You appear to have been very busy during the time you were in France.'

Paige laughed and went back to her seat, picked up her drink. 'And why not? From what I've heard I must have led a very dull life before.'

'It wasn't all dull.'

'Do you mean my so terribly exciting engagement to you? I suppose you think a few rough kisses sufficient to have a woman drooling over you. You couldn't be more wrong.' She looked at him from under her lashes. 'I don't find you at all romantic.'

'Ah, romantic! A very evocative word.' Crossing the room, Milo refilled his glass. 'You know, Paige, the way you keep harping on about how unexciting I am only convinces me that you'd really like more of the same.'

She gave a disbelieving laugh, drained her glass and rose gracefully. 'What an egotist you are. Won't anything get through to you? This is all very boring. I'm going to bed.'

'Running away, Paige?' His voice was soft but challenging.

Her face suddenly becoming tense, she said, 'I did it before, why not again?'

She saw his hands clench, but he could find nothing to say. Their eyes met, emotions naked in their gaze. But Paige quickly looked away, picked up her cape and ran upstairs to her room.

Which of them had lain awake the longest during that night was impossible to tell when they met in the kitchen the next morning. Paige had certainly found sleep elusive as she'd tried to get used to the strange bed, the strange room, and this even stranger life. And to make some sense of the chaotic thoughts and pictures that chased through her aching head. Milo, too, had shadows around his eyes, as if the thought of her being so near and yet so distant from him had robbed him of any rest. It was Saturday so he didn't have to work, and he was wearing casual clothes, an open-necked shirt under a sweater. He was already fixing his own breakfast when Paige came down. She was wearing a long sarong-style skirt and a loose V-necked sweater, the sleeves pushed up her arms, but still managed to look chic.

'Good morning. Did you sleep OK?' Milo asked.

Her eyes scanned his face, and she thought she saw tension from their confrontation of the night before in the tightness of his mouth, but she decided to ignore it, the better to hide her own. 'Like a log,' she lied. 'I feel marvellous.'

'I'm glad to hear it,' he said on a sardonic note, adding, 'I wonder if you'll still be saying the same thing after you've seen your grandmother today?'

Paige laughed. 'I see you're trying to spoil my day before it's hardly begun.'

His face relaxed a little. 'Help yourself to whatever you want. There's eggs and bacon and orange juice in the fridge.'

Rooting through the cupboards, Paige said, 'Didn't you say you have a housekeeper or something to look after you?'

'Yes, but she doesn't work at the weekends. I'm quite capable of looking after myself.'

Finding a bowl, Paige poured some cereal into it. 'Am I supposed to go back to the house in Chelsea to meet my grandmother?'

'No, I rang yesterday evening and told her you were here.'

'And did you tell her why?'

Sitting down at the table, Milo poured orange juice into a glass. 'Yes,' he said evenly.

Paige was immediately intrigued. Coming to sit opposite him, she said, 'And what did she say when she knew her dear friend the Major was just a dirty old pervert?'

'That's rather a strong way of putting it.'

'He deserves it. So what did she say?'

'She didn't make any comment. It seems that Mrs Davieson had already been on to her, giving her their explanation.'

'Which was?'

'She didn't say.'

'I bet she doesn't tell us,' Paige said reflectively.

'You seem to be well acquainted with your grandmother's personality,' Milo commented, watching her.

With a laugh, she said, 'Would you tell anyone if your old friend had spun you a lot of lies? Of course not. And stop trying to catch me out.'

'Was that what I was doing?'

Putting her elbow on the table, she rested her chin on her hand. She had tied her hair back today and hadn't yet made up her face. She looked much younger, much more innocent. 'You know you were. Don't you trust me, Milo?'

'As you pointed out yesterday, you're a stranger. How can I possibly know whether I can trust you or not?'

She gave a rich laugh. 'Hoist with my own argument! How unfair—but what a typically male answer. Throw the ball back in the woman's own court; that's what men do all the time.'

'You would seem to have a low opinion of my sex.'

'Oh, no. Men are men. They can't help it, the poor things.'

He grinned at the pity in her tone. 'Your grand-mother won't be here until nearly lunchtime. Is there anything you'd like to do this morning?'

'Yes, I'd like to see over this house. If that's OK?'

'Of course. Explore as you like.'

'Won't you show me round?'

His glance flicked to her face, but Milo merely nod-ded and said, 'If you like. After breakfast.'

They cleared up between them, Paige trying to be helpful but just getting in the way. She picked up a couple of plates, turned, and bumped into him. For a brief moment their bodies were touching. Instinctively Milo put a hand on her arm to steady her. His skin wasn't hot but somehow his touch seemed to sear into her, making Paige's heart suddenly race. The kiss, his fiercely compulsive embrace of last night, filled their minds. She flinched away from him and Milo's face hardened. Exasperatedly, he said, 'Here, let me do it.'

He took the plates from her, put them in the dish-washer, then cleared the rest of the things from the table.

'Sorry. It's just that I don't know where anything goes,' she said pointedly when he'd finished.

Milo raised a sardonic eyebrow. 'You don't have to spell it out; I've already got the message.'

'So pleased,' she said with a grin. Picking up the paper, she began to glance through it, then came to a stop at an inside page.

'Have you looked at the paper yet?' she asked.

'Yes,' Milo replied evenly.

'And did you see this piece about me?'

'Yes, although it's pure supposition,' he said, switching on the dishwasher.

'They haven't lost any time in finding out that I'm back—or in linking my name to yours.'

'As the last news they have of you is that we were about to be married, they're bound to do that.'

Paige tossed the paper aside. 'I suppose so.' She smiled at his broad back. 'They'll have a field day when they find out about Jean-Louis.'

Turning to face her, Milo leaned against the work-top and folded his arms. 'If they find out,' he agreed.

'Aren't they likely to?'

'Not unless you tell them. I certainly shan't. And the only other person who knows is Charles Readman, who certainly won't betray any secrets.'

'What about my grandmother?'

Milo laughed. 'Talking to the gutter press is the last thing she'd do.'

Tilting her head, she studied him for a moment. 'You don't want anyone to find out about me and Jean-Louis, do you?'

'Naturally not. Or that you lost your memory. All sorts of people could try and take advantage of you if it was found out.'

'In what way?'

'Saying that you owed them money. That they were friends of yours.' He shrugged. 'Use your imagination.'

'I don't like the idea of that.'

'So, when the press track you down, refuse to speak to them.'

Paige brightened. 'What a good job I moved out of the flat; they'll never find me here.'

'I shouldn't bank on it,' Milo said wryly. 'They almost camped outside the place when you first disappeared. What little they could find out about you they printed, what they couldn't they made up. And they illustrated the items with what seemed like every photograph you'd ever had taken.'

'Really?' Paige smiled gleefully. 'I hope they were good photos.'

His eyebrows flew up, then Milo burst out laughing. 'I'm beginning to think you've become incorrigible.'

She smiled back at him. 'Of course.'

Suddenly the tension between them was gone. Getting to her feet, Paige said, 'You promised to show me the house.'

Milo did so at a leisurely pace when he saw that she was really interested. The house was beautiful and full of pictures. 'I bet you have an underground vault full of masterpieces,' she teased.

'No, pictures are to be looked at, to be loved.' He was standing in front of a Dutch painting of a vase of flowers, the drops of dew still glistening on their petals. It was exquisitely painted; you felt that if you got close you would be able to smell the perfume that still lingered on the roses. Milo was standing with his hands in his pockets, looking up at it with eyes full of admiration and warmth.

'As you say, you love the paintings,' Paige observed tightly.

Something in her voice made him turn his head to look at her. 'Yes, but paintings, after all, are only things. Inanimate objects. The love I felt for you transcends anything I might feel for the whole collection of pictures.'

He had got his tenses mixed up, Paige realised. He had used first the past tense, then the present. She wondered if his feelings for her were as mixed. He had loved her, but now he didn't know whether he did or not. Personally she wasn't at all sure that he had ever loved her, even though he'd said so. Wanted her—perhaps. Wanted to combine the two families for the sake of the company—definitely. But love? Did he even know what it was? Maybe he'd convinced himself that was what he'd felt for her, because it would have been so convenient to do so. She gave a small smile and turned away, refusing to be drawn into any deep discussion, anything that might lead to him kissing her again.

There was a basement in the house, but Milo didn't use it to store pictures. Instead he had turned it into what almost amounted to a sports complex. There was an indoor pool, a gym, and a sauna. 'How wonderful!' Paige exclaimed. 'No wonder you look so fit.'

'Working out helps to take your mind off your problems. And it helps to ease frustration, too.'

His voice was heavy with meaning, but Paige refused to be intimidated. Lifting her chin, she said, 'I'll have to try it some time, then—now that I'm away from Jean-Louis.'

'Do you have to keep throwing him in my face?' he said tiredly.

'It's your own fault. You shouldn't keep doing it.'

'Doing what?'

'Trying to make me responsible for all your—troubles. If you're frustrated it's your own fault. You should have found someone else.'

She went to turn and go on, but Milo reached out and caught her wrist. His face very tense, he said, 'Please don't insult me by ever making that suggestion again.'

His eyes seemed to bore into her, but Paige said, 'If you expect me to believe that you've been living like a monk, you must be crazy.'

'Don't judge me by the standards set by your Frenchmen, Paige. You're the only woman I wanted.' He gave a thin smile. 'When you know that you've met your ideal, why settle for anything less?'

'Your ideal woman!' She gave a disbelieving laugh. 'I don't buy that. You're a man of the world, Milo. You've been around. You must have known loads of women.'

'Perhaps. In the past. But what I said still stands.'

'I still don't believe it.'

'Don't you?' A bleak look came into his grey eyes. 'No, perhaps you don't. What do you know of the devastation of mind and heart that a man feels when the woman he loves walks out on him? The dread and the fear when you think that she's been taken, may be injured or dead. The pain and hurt when her car is found and it becomes clear that she's gone of her own accord, without even a word of explanation. The nights when you lie awake torturing your mind with wondering why—why!' His voice grew fierce, vehement.

'And how would you know what it's like to have to send back wedding presents, to cancel arrangements, to tell well-meaning friends that she's gone, that you don't know where she is? How do you take the pity in their faces? How do you listen to the remarks behind your back, deal with conversations that break off when you walk into a room?' His grip on her wrist tightened unmercifully. 'And just how the hell do you cope with having your wedding day come around with no ceremony, without the marriage you've been longing for? And how do you get through the long hours that should have been your wedding night, alone, rejected, frustrated out of your mind?' He shook her suddenly. 'Well, how do you? How do you?'

With appalled eyes and pale cheeks, Paige stared up into his face. She'd had no idea of his depth of feeling, that he was even capable of such intensity, such abject despair. There was a lot she could have said in retaliation, but now wasn't the time to say it. There might never be a time. So instead she just shook her head. 'I—didn't know you felt like that.'

Milo took a breath and let her go, brushed his hair back from his forehead. 'No, how could you? I'm sorry.'

He walked on, stood in front of the next picture, but Paige stayed where she was for a few moments, looking at his set profile, at the drawn features. Her heart was deeply troubled; she had had no idea of his suffering, of the torment she had unwittingly caused. Becoming aware that she hadn't followed him, Milo glanced towards her. Immediately she avoided his eyes, coming to stand beside him and making some facetious remark about the portrait in front of her. Behind her Milo half lifted a hand to put it on her shoulder, then dropped it to his side, his face grim.

They were more subdued for the rest of the tour, and Paige was sure that Milo cut it short. Afterwards he said he had some phone calls to make and went into his study, so she wandered out into the garden. But as she strolled down the lawns near the driveway someone shouted her name and Paige saw that there were several reporters and cameramen crowding against the gate. Quickly she turned and walked behind a screening hedge of bushes, then went round to the back of the house where there were high trees.

But she felt vulnerable even here, and kept glancing uneasily at the high old wall that ran round the property, afraid that an enterprising cameraman might scale it and take her photo. It occurred to her that this was what Milo must have gone through all those months ago. It was hard to imagine what it must have been like, especially as she'd disappeared so close to their wedding, and especially if he'd really cared about her as he'd said he had. She as good as believed now that that was true. It would have taken superb acting to have feigned that outburst earlier.

The sun came out and Paige found a stone bench and sat down, tilted back her head, feeling its warmth on her face. A great tide of guilt engulfed her and tears pricked at her eyes. Angrily she tried to shake it off. Milo was nothing to her. Nothing! But the stupid stab of guilt wouldn't go away.

'Paige?'

Opening her eyes quickly, she turned to see Milo standing quite close by. He had come across the lawn from the kitchen and she hadn't heard him.

'You're crying,' he said roughly.

She laughed. 'The sun's strong; it was hurting my eyes.'

'Now, I wonder why I don't believe you?'

'Well, one thing's for sure,' she said derisively. 'If I am crying it certainly isn't over you.'

'Of course not,' he agreed smoothly. 'But it's interesting to find that you're not the tough, uncaring person you pretend to be.'

'That's right. A hidden heart of gold, that's me.' Her tone was flippant, hiding the dismay she felt at being caught out. 'Just like a marshmallow teacake: hard on the outside and soft as butter within.'

Milo grinned as he was meant to do. 'I came to tell you your grandmother has arrived.'

'Oh.' Slowly she got up and walked beside him back to the house.

'She's waiting for you in the drawing-room,' he told her when they reached the hall.

He went to turn away but she caught his sleeve, saying nervously, 'Where are you going? You'll stay, surely?'

'She wants to see you alone.'

'Well, I'd rather you were there.' She gave him an entreating look, but Milo shook his head and walked away.

Damn him, then, she thought, and strode purposefully across the hall and pushed open the door.

Her grandmother was exactly as she had imagined she would be. A tall, thin, very upright woman with iron-grey hair cut short and neat. She was standing by the fireplace with a closed expression on her face. There was no cry of welcome, no smile. The elderly woman's eyes merely went over her and she nodded. 'So you've decided to come home at last,' she said curtly.

Paige looked at her for a long moment then walked across the room and held out her hand. 'I take it you're Mrs Chandos. How do you do? I'm told I'm your granddaughter.' Her tone was very polite, very distant.

The hard features didn't soften any. 'Are you trying to tell me that you have really lost your memory?'

'I'm not trying to tell you anything,' Paige said calmly. 'It was you who asked for this meeting, not me.'

'You have certainly changed,' her grandmother said shortly. 'You would never have spoken to me in such a manner in the past.'

'Really?' Paige was visibly uninterested.

'But I'm not at all sure that I believe you. However—' she gave a shrug '—if that is what you wish me to accept, then I have little choice. Milo tells me that he found you in France?'

'Yes.'

'What were you doing there?'

'I was working as a waitress in a café in Paris.'

The eyebrows went up. 'Perhaps it did you good, although I always tried not to spoil you.'

'I'm sure you didn't,' Paige remarked.

A pair of shrewd eyes looked into hers. 'You've found some spirit, it seems. Now that you're back, I'm sure you'll want to return to your old life. As it appears that the flat I bought you in Chelsea isn't available at the moment, I shall take you back to Lancashire with me.'

So that was all that was to be said about the Major, was it? Paige realised in amazement. She gasped inwardly and almost laughed aloud at the older woman's ability to ignore the incident. Did she go through her life sweeping any nastiness under the carpet? Keeping her tone brisk and businesslike, Paige said, 'I do not wish to go to Lancashire with you. Or anywhere else,' she added quickly as she saw Mrs Chandos open her mouth to speak. 'I intend to sell the house in Chelsea *with its spyhole in the bathroom ceiling*,' she emphasised. 'And as soon as the legal side of things is taken care of I shall go back to France.'

'Will you, indeed? And what is so attractive about being a waitress in Paris, may I ask?'

'You should rather ask, What is there that is attractive in England? And the answer is nothing.'

'What about Milo? He is your fiancé.'

'He may have been. He is no longer.'

'Is he still willing to marry you?'

Her voice chill, Paige said, 'I have no idea. As I said, there is nothing to keep me here.'

'Whether you really have amnesia or not, you'd be a fool to just walk away from marrying him.'

'I'll be a fool, then.'

Her grandmother's face tightened. 'He is extremely fond of you, you know.'

'Really?' Paige's voice was cold as ice.

'Don't try and freeze me out, girl; it was me who taught you how.'

'Somehow I think I should have guessed that.'

The old lady looked at her for a moment, then turned towards the ornate, gold-framed mirror over the mantelpiece. She seemed to hesitate as she stared unseeingly at her own reflection, then made up her mind. 'You're angry; I can see that. And if you have forgotten your old life then you're probably very confused. But I am here to help you, in any way I can.'

'Thank you. But I hardly think that you—' Paige broke off as an idea occurred to her, and she looked searchingly at the older woman. 'Do you mean that?'

'I wouldn't have said it unless I meant it,' Mrs Chandos said shortly. 'I am not the sort of woman who mouths constant platitudes. You should know that.' She gave an impatient wave of her hand. 'But no, if you've forgotten me then you wouldn't know. How can I help you?'

'Were you in my confidence?'

'I'm happy to believe so, yes.'

'Did I tell you why I ran away?'

There was the smallest flicker of hesitation before Mrs Chandos said, 'No.'

'I didn't come to see you before I left? Ring you? Or *anything*?'

Again the hesitation. 'No, you did none of those things.'

'So it seems that you weren't in my confidence, then.'

After a long moment her grandmother sighed. 'No, you didn't tell me, but I do know why. When your car was found at the airport, your diary was there among the things you'd left. As your next of kin it was given to me, and I read it.'

'Will you tell me what it said?' Her eyes fixed on the other woman's face, Paige moved to stand behind a chair and gripped its back.

'You left because of a mistake. You had been mis-informed.' Her tone became remonstrative. 'But, in-stead of acting like a sensible being and checking it out, you let your emotions overwhelm you and took the silly, melodramatic action of running away. To France as it turns out. Leaving—'

'Save the recriminations for some other time,' Paige interrupted. 'Just tell me what you found out.'

Her grandmother looked affronted at her tone, but said, 'You were very much in love with Milo. You hero-worshipped him as much as anything. And it was an ideal match; everyone thought so. I certainly did. You had been worried at first that it had something to do with the company, but he had convinced you that he loved you for yourself. But then some—inter-fering busybody told you some malicious lies that greatly upset you.'

'What lies?'

'It really isn't necessary for you to know. All that matters is that they were lies and you were wrong to have run away. I'm sure that—'

'Will you please stop treating me like a child?' Paige broke in angrily. 'What lies?'

Mrs Chandos looked taken aback for a minute, then gave a sigh. 'Very well, if you must have it. You were told that Milo had a mistress. That it was a relationship that had been going on for some time and that it would continue after your marriage. Absolute nonsense, of course. But from what you had written in your diary it upset you terribly. You seemed heartbroken by it.'

So that was it, thought Paige. Added to her past doubts about Milo's true feelings for her, finding that out would have been enough to make anyone take off, to look for space in which to think things through. So he'd had a mistress, had he? And here he was now, swearing undying love. The hypocrite. 'How do you know it was nonsense?' she asked. 'It may have been true.'

'It wasn't,' she was told shortly. 'I made it my business to find out. There was no truth in it whatsoever.' Mrs Chandos's tone altered a little. 'Milo is, of course, experienced; what man isn't these days? But his feelings for you were absolutely genuine. He fell head over heels in love with you almost from the moment he saw you after I brought you back from India.' There was a note of satisfaction in her voice, that of a matchmaker who thought she'd engineered the perfect match. 'When you disappeared he was completely devastated.'

'So he tells me.'

Her grandmother looked at her sharply. 'If you take my advice you'll—'

'I won't,' Paige broke in. 'So please don't give it. In the diary, did it say who told me that Milo had a mistress?'

'It seems that you received an anonymous letter.

Why you should choose to believe it is beyond my comprehension, but—'

'What did the letter say? Was it quoted?'

Grudgingly Mrs Chandos said, 'It was actually enclosed in the diary.'

Paige's eyebrows rose. 'Was it? And what did it say?'

'More or less what I have told you.'

'More or less?' Paige looked at her stiff face closely. 'But I think that there must have been more to make me so convinced. What was it?'

Her lips tightening, the old lady said, 'It said that if you wanted proof you should go to a restaurant at a certain time and you would see Milo there with his mistress.'

'I see. And presumably I did this?'

'Yes. As I said, you appeared to have been heartbroken by it. But why you chose to run away instead of coming to me, I fail to see. We could quite easily have sorted out the whole thing and—'

'It's in the past,' Paige said shortly. She gave the older woman a keen look. 'The first thing Milo asked me when he found me was why had I run away. Do I take it that you didn't tell him about this letter?'

'No. It wasn't found until some weeks after you disappeared, and I wanted to check on the facts for myself. I hired a detective to find out. But it was some time before it could be proved that there was nothing to find out. It's always harder to prove innocence than guilt in these matters, it seems. By then so much time had passed that the letter seemed irrelevant set against your continued disappearance. And, of course, I daily expected you to come to your senses and return home, when I could have convinced you that the accusation was all a lie.'

'You said that Milo was devastated by my running out on him; didn't it occur to you that by leaving the diary behind I was explaining why I had gone? Don't you think he had a right to know?'

Mrs Chandos sniffed. 'If you must know, Milo and I had a quarrel after you went and before the diary was found. He said—and it was completely unjustified—that I had driven you away. That I had interfered in your life once too often. Whereas I felt that he must have tried to push you into—into something you weren't ready for. I still think so.'

Paige frowned in puzzlement. 'But I thought you wanted me to marry him.'

'Of course I did. But you were only twenty and had led a sheltered life; I felt that you needed a much longer engagement before the wedding. But Milo insisted on bringing the date forward. And I'm not sure he was willing to wait until then,' she said with some indignation.

Paige's face cleared and she laughed. 'Good heavens, you mean sex.'

'Quite.'

The old lady sniffed again and Paige had a sudden insight into what a miserable childhood her own mother must have had. No wonder she had fallen for foreigners, especially the Argentinian who had whisked her off to his native country. 'Do you still have the diary and the letter?' she asked.

'Yes, but not with me. They're at home in Lancashire.'

'I would like to have them.'

'Very well. I suppose you are entitled to know what happened to you.' She hesitated, then said again, 'Will you come with me now?'

'No.'

The old lady looked at her for a moment, then picked up her bag. 'I see that there is no point in my talking to you. Are you going to stay here?'

'My plans are undecided.'

'I see.' She nodded her head in acknowledgement and walked slowly to the door, limping a little.

Paige watched her, thinking that one could almost feel sorry for the old dear, but she said nothing.

At the door Mrs Chandos turned. 'No matter what happens, Paige, even if we never see one another again, you will always be my grandchild. Nothing can change that. And Milo wasn't the only one whose life was shattered when you ran away.' Then she let herself out, and Paige heard her footsteps slowly crossing the hall.

The footsteps stopped and she heard her grandmother speak to Milo. Whatever it was, the conversation was brief, because shortly afterwards came the sound of the front door opening and closing. Then Milo's brisk footsteps crossing the hall towards her. Paige braced her shoulders, expecting a tirade, but when Milo came in he didn't seem at all angry.

'I gather you won't be leaving with your grandmother?'

'No. The whole idea sounded extremely boring.' Paige sat down in a chair, crossed her legs. 'But I think I'd better move into a hotel.'

'Why?'

'People will start talking about us if I stay here.'

'Let them,' Milo said dismissively.

'Yes, but it will probably be reported in the papers and I'd hate anyone to get the wrong idea.'

'What they think is their business.'

'You don't get the point,' Paige said sweetly. 'Jean-Louis might get the wrong idea.'

'I see.' Milo stood looking down at her contempla-tively. 'You know something, Paige? I don't care if he does—and I don't think you really care either.'

'Of course I care.'

'So phone him up and explain that you're staying here because if you went to a hotel you would be hounded by the press.'

'You think I would be?' she asked with some mis-givings.

'Of course.'

'I'd better stay, then.' She looked at him from un-der her lashes, said deliberately, 'Although I should hate to cramp your style.'

Leaning against the mantelpiece—a habitual pose, it seemed—Milo folded his arms. 'And what is that supposed to mean?'

Paige shrugged. 'Presumably you have some social life. I don't want to get in the way.'

'You would never be in the way, in any aspect of my life.'

His positive and immediate reply made her blink, but she said, 'Oh, but I could think of somewhere I would most definitely be in the way.'

'Then you are thinking along the wrong lines.'

'Am I?' Her voice lost its sarcastic note, became vulnerable.

'Most definitely.' Taking a stride towards her, Milo came down onto his knees beside her chair. His face intent, he took hold of her hand as he said, 'As far as I'm concerned nothing has changed. I still feel the same way about you as I always did. I'm crazy about you, and I always will be. Please tell me you believe that.'

Her eyes very large in a face gone suddenly pale, Paige studied him, trying to see into his mind, to decide whether she could trust him. Then she remembered what her grandmother had told her and her expression changed, grew infinitely mocking. 'Why, Milo, how romantic! Tell me, have you gone down on your knees to propose to me all over again?'

His mouth tightened. 'Don't belittle my feelings for you, Paige. They go far too deep for that. And I don't think you can possibly have changed so much that you'd be cruel enough to ridicule them.'

'That's emotional blackmail.'

'It wasn't meant to be.'

'Good, because it would never have worked. I have absolutely no emotions as far as you're concerned.' She smiled, and there was malice in it. 'So I can be just as cruel, as you call it, as I like.'

Milo's face had grown taut, but his voice was steady as he said, 'If you have no feelings for me, then why bother to try and hurt me?'

Leaning back in the chair, Paige tilted her head to one side and pouted her lips as she contemplated him. 'Because it amuses me, of course.'

As soon as the words were out she knew it had been the wrong thing to say. A flash of white-hot anger showed in his eyes. 'It amuses you to play with the emotions of someone you claim you don't even know?' he demanded harshly.

Pushing him aside, Paige got to her feet and swung round to face him as he rose with her. 'Yes, it amuses me! And I'll tell you why. You keep on about me running away, but a girl doesn't run away from the man she loves unless—' She broke off, said shortly, 'Oh, what the hell does it matter?'

She would have walked away but Milo caught hold of her. 'Unless what? Finish what you were going to say,' he insisted.

For a moment she resisted but felt his grip tighten, so spread her hands and said, 'All right. All right. A woman wouldn't leave the man she loves unless she found out that he was lying to her, deceiving her. I didn't run away. You *drove* me away.'

'How can you possibly think that?' he said roughly.

'It stands to reason. The thought of marrying you became so unbearable that I couldn't face it.' She glared up at him, then added, 'I must have had to get away. Maybe I intended to come back when I'd had time and space to think things through. I don't know.' She paused, then said vehemently, 'But you knew. You above everyone else knew why I left—must have known. So why don't you stop pretending and tell me?'

'There was no reason. None! I still don't know why you went.'

Paige didn't believe him, was convinced he must have at least suspected, and said hotly, 'In that case you should talk to my grandmother. She gave me ample reason for ditching you.'

She felt his hand tremble as he clutched her arm. 'What did she say to you?'

Suddenly certainty left her as she looked into his eyes and saw torment there. Not hurt pride, not anger, but bleak despair. In a voice that was so ragged it sounded unlike her own, Paige said, 'She told me you had a mistress—no, that's wrong; she said I'd been told you had a mistress. That it was a long-standing affair, and that you had every intention of carrying on with it after—after our marriage. That was, I think, justification enough for walking out on you. Don't you agree?'

Milo took a long time to answer her. He just stared down into her face before giving a long sigh and letting go of her arm. 'So that was it,' he said, his voice so low that she hardly heard it.

Paige waited for him to go on, then impatiently asked again, 'Well? Don't you think it was cause enough?'

His reply completely threw her. 'Yes. More than enough. If you felt so insecure that you believed it. But you obviously didn't love me enough to trust me.' He moved away and looked out of the window, then spoke with his back to her as he said, 'You said that you'd been told. Who told you?'

'My grandmother said that I'd received an anonymous letter. Evidently it was enclosed in a diary that I'd left in my car.'

'So she's known all along?'

'Yes.'

'The old witch.' Milo swore softly. 'She can't resist meddling in other people's lives and trying to control them. What exactly did she tell you?'

Paige repeated what she'd been told and watched his face gradually become grimmer. 'Of course I haven't read the diary; I'm only telling you what she said.'

He nodded, turned to face her. 'About a week before you did your vanishing act I too received a letter. From an old girlfriend—or so I believed. It said that she was in trouble and would I meet her for lunch. I

was reluctant to do so, but was unable to contact her.'
He gave a shrug. 'And, besides, we'd had some good
times together in the past. I felt I owed it to her at
least to listen, and see if I was able to help.' Milo
glanced at Paige. 'And the fact that I'd fallen head
over heels for the girl I'd been waiting for all my life
didn't mean that I had to ignore a past friendship.'

'Friendship?' Paige queried, her brows lifting.

'All right. An ex-lover, then.'

'Tell me, are there many of them around?'

But he ignored that and went on, 'She was there at
the restaurant, but she said that she had also received
a letter, purporting to be from me, asking her to a
farewell lunch before my marriage. A get-together for
old times' sake,' he said dryly.

'Didn't you suspect anything?' Paige queried.

'Yes. I thought that she'd sent the letter to me and
that her letter didn't exist. I thought she was playing
some game of her own. So I cut the meeting short.
Ducked out on the lunch and left.'

'Do you think she could have sent the anonymous
letter to me?'

Again he shrugged, but it was an angry one this
time. 'I don't know. It's possible, I suppose. And I
have enemies; you make them in business. Marrying
you would have made me a lot more powerful in the
City. Any business rival might have come up with the
scheme in an effort to break up the marriage. And it
worked—better than they could have dared to hope,'
he added bitterly.

'But how would they have known about your relationship with this woman?'

'It wasn't exactly a secret. We were both single so
there was no reason for it to be. She's an executive
with a company we deal with, so anyone in Caine and

Chandos, or a rival in the commercial world, could easily have known.' He gave an impatient gesture that for a moment reminded Paige of Jean-Louis. 'But we'd parted before you came on the scene and I'd hardly seen her since.'

'You parted as friends?'

'It was a bit one-sided,' Milo admitted ruefully. 'She started to get serious, but I found I wasn't that interested.'

'Do you think she might have done it out of spite? The ''woman scorned'' thing?'

'Perhaps. And I intend to find out,' he said forcefully.

Paige looked at him for a moment, then said, 'Don't bother. Forget it. After all, it hardly matters now, does it?'

But Milo, his tone fierce, said, 'You were made so miserable that you ran away, and I have been living in hell for over a year, and you say it doesn't matter? Of course it damn well matters!'

'To you, perhaps.' Her voice grew mocking. 'I can see you lost a lot by it. But I'm glad it happened. It seems to have done me a big favour. From what I can gather, I must have led an extremely restricted and boring life. Tied to that dragon of a grandmother. Engaged to a man I wasn't sure of, who I suspected of wanting me only for the power I could give him— and who was also a womaniser on top of everything else.' Paige watched him as she spoke, adding each word as if it were the flick of a whip and expecting to enjoy seeing him flinch. But then she suddenly turned away. 'I was well out of it,' she said abruptly. 'So if you do any searching you must do it on your own account, not mine.'

She went to open the door but Milo suddenly

grabbed her and slammed her back against it, putting a hand on either side of her, his body so close that she couldn't move. 'Who was it who taught you to become so sadistic?' he demanded roughly.

Paige stared at him, taken aback by his vehemence. She was surprised by it but not frightened. 'Maybe it was you,' she retorted after a moment.

'Don't be ridiculous!'

Stung, she said, 'No, not so ridiculous. When a girl hero-worships a man and then finds that he's done the dirty on her, that he's lied to her and deceived her, it's enough to change anyone.' Her green eyes flashed fire and defiance. 'Maybe I was meek and mild and vulnerable before, but I'm not now. I may have been in awe of you once, but now I see you for what you are—as greedy for power as the next man. The charm you turned on doesn't work any more, Milo. I see through you.'

'The only lying that's been done is by you—to yourself,' he said curtly. Adding forcefully, 'I have *never* lied to you.' His angry eyes blazed into hers. 'It wasn't my fault if you put me on some kind of a pedestal. I tried to talk to you, to put you at ease and make our relationship a more equal one. But your grandmother had put all sorts of silly, old-fashioned ideas in your head about marriage—and about men. No man could live up to the standard you'd dreamed up for me. I was human, Paige. A normal man with normal experiences of life.'

'And of women!'

'Yes, of course of women. I'm no saint.'

'Obviously.'

She tried to push him aside, but Milo held her back against the door again. 'No, you're going to hear me out. You were young for your age. Impressionable.

You wanted a fairy-tale romance and that letter destroyed it for you. OK, I'm sorry. But don't you realise how much of a coward you were to run away instead of trying to sort it out? To just leave like that without a word? All right, so you'd been hurt, but did you think for one moment of the hurt you were causing to the people who loved you by disappearing the way you did?' Before she could speak he made a disparaging noise. 'But no, of course you didn't. You were too busy thinking about yourself to give a thought to anyone else. So maybe you always were a cruel little cow!'

Paige looked at him, her face tight. 'You're talking to me as if I should remember how I felt then. I don't. I can only guess at my feelings. Maybe it was the letter that made me hate you, maybe it was something else. I don't know.'

'But you do know that you hated me.' Milo's voice was raw.

Slowly Paige said, 'Yes. Somehow, from the moment I saw you in Paris, I knew that I hated you.' She paused for a second then said, 'You accuse me of being unfeeling, of hurting you when you loved me. But if I'd been convinced that you loved me then surely I wouldn't have gone? It was knowing that you didn't care that drove me away. And as for my grandmother being hurt—from what I've seen she's about as sensitive as a tank; I don't think that anything could hurt her.'

'Then you are very blind. She doted on you. OK, she was completely misguided, and didn't do you any favours. But she brought you up in the way she thought was right. She wanted to protect you and make sure you didn't make any mistakes. But that doesn't mean that she didn't love you with all her heart.'

Her voice bitter, Paige said, 'It's a strange, un-healthy kind of love that restricts you, wants to shape your life for you, refuses to let you have anything to do with your natural parents. I'd call that oppression, not love.'

Milo put a hand on her shoulder. 'You seem very conversant suddenly with the way you were brought up.'

'Of course I am. I've just today met the person responsible for it. Anyone with any intelligence could see immediately what kind of a person she was—is.' She gave a short laugh. 'I don't think that I could ever have stood up to her before; she certainly seemed surprised by it.'

'Oh, yes, you're full of surprises.'

Milo's tone was dry, almost bitter. His hand was still on her shoulder and she could feel the heat of it through her clothes, feel the tension in him. Her mind went back to his ruthless embrace of the night before, and Paige looked at his face for a long moment, her expressive eyes dwelling on his mouth, the lean hand-someness of his features. Then she said, her voice slightly unsteady, 'Please don't touch me.'

As he removed his hand from her shoulder, Milo's face grew sardonic. 'I beg your pardon.'

Ignoring the heavy sarcasm in his voice, she said, 'Because I want to ask you something.'

'What is it?'

'Were we lovers?'

At last it was out in the open, the question that had been between them, which made everything else seem trivial in comparison. The three words hung in the air as Milo stiffened, stared down at her. She had taken him by surprise as she'd intended, but apart from the initial shock his face gave little away. He blinked, and it was a full minute before he said heavily, 'Yes.'

Paige swallowed, found it suddenly difficult to breathe. She turned her head away from his gaze and when she could speak kept her voice light, almost flippant, as she said, 'Really? And was it good?'

Putting a hand under her chin, Milo made her face him. His eyes, dark and intent, studied her. 'What do you think?' he said silkily.

Her voice unsteady, she laughed again. 'How should I know? From what I've learnt about my past, I was so unworldly that it was probably terrible. Was it?' Her heart was beating loudly in her chest and Paige began to wish she had never asked, but despite her misgivings she was fascinated and had to know.

Lifting his head, Milo looked down at her as if considering his answer. Then he said, 'You were unworldly and nervous, yes—the first time. But far from frigid. Once you had learned to relax, you proved to be more than responsive. Beneath that naive, rather prim exterior there was a sensuous and very receptive woman just waiting to be aroused.' And he deliberately let his hand glide down her cheek to her neck and then on down to caress her breast.

Page caught her breath as her eyes, huge now, stared into his. Then she lifted her hand and knocked his away. 'Just because I found you persuasive in the past doesn't mean that you can do the same now.'

Milo gave a small crooked smile. 'Of course not. I was forgetting.'

Ducking under his arm, she took a few steps away, then turned to face him. 'You said "the first time"; does that mean that we—we were lovers for some time?'

He hesitated, then said, 'No, not for very long.'

'And it wasn't so good that it kept me here. I still took off.'

With a slight shrug, he said, 'Maybe it was because it was so good that you ran away. You couldn't bear to think that there might be someone else, that you might have to—share me.'

Paige's eyes widened, then she said venomously, 'You are an arrogant, conceited bastard! You don't deserve that any woman should love you. I certainly don't, and I can only feel infinite pity for any woman who's stupid enough to care about you. Now, get out of my way!' Pushing him aside, she pulled open the door and stormed out of the room.

Going up to her room, Paige changed into smarter clothes and made up her face. When she came downstairs again Milo, who was sitting in the drawing-room with the door open, saw her and came into the hall.

'Going out?'

'As you see,' she said stiffly.

'Would you like me to drive you somewhere?'

'No, thanks.'

'The press are still outside,' he reminded her.

'Then I'll call a cab.'

She expected him to argue, but Milo just said, 'OK. You'll find a number by the phone.'

He walked back into the drawing-room and Paige watched him go with mixed feelings. When the cab came she directed it to drop her at Leicester Square, and went to a cinema. It seemed strange to watch a film in English without subtitles and to hear English being spoken all around her. She seemed to have been in France so long, but already it was a world away. Fleetingly she thought about Jean-Louis, and wondered if he would try to phone her this evening, but soon her mind went back to Milo and his admission that they'd been lovers.

To hear him say so had come as a great shock. She had been sure that he would deny it. Paige had hoped, by asking the question, to clear the air between them, to make the situation less tense. But it had only served to have the opposite effect. Now the stress of being in close proximity to him would increase. He might try to touch her again as he had earlier, as if he had the right to do so. That angered Paige; he had no rights over her, and she'd made it more than clear that she wasn't interested. No matter what he'd said had happened between them in the past.

On the screen there was a love scene, a couple in bed together. Paige felt her cheeks start to burn as she wondered what it would be like to be made love to by Milo. He'd implied that she'd been unawakened, that his lovemaking had worked a small miracle and made a sensual woman out of a naive girl. Paige didn't buy that. She might have been held down with an iron hand by her grandmother but she couldn't have been completely naive, surely? Maybe it hadn't been like that at all. Maybe Milo had told her what he wanted her to believe. The male actor ran his hand up the bare leg of the actress; there was a glimpse of naked shoulders, a thigh, of a masculine chest, as they began to writhe on the bed.

Milo as a lover. She thought of him doing the same things to her, could almost feel the heat of his hand on her skin. She had no doubt that he could arouse her if he wanted to, that he was experienced enough to more than satisfy any woman. Her chest felt tight, her throat dry. The lovers on the screen were panting with desire, groaning, kissing. Paige felt a sudden and very fierce surge of longing deep inside, a yearning so fierce it made her gasp. Cheeks blazing, she abruptly got up and left the cinema, hurried out into air that was cool even if it was loaded with pollution from the traffic.

She paused for a moment on the pavement, trying to recover, but this was no place for a woman on her own to hang around, and she plunged into the nearest restaurant and ordered a meal, sitting at a table in the rear of the place with her back to the room. As soon as she got back to Milo's house she would phone Jean-Louis, she decided, and maybe she would think again about moving to a hotel. After her meal Paige bought an evening paper and read it in the taxi going back to Hampstead, then wished she hadn't when she saw her own photograph, taken by some enterprising photographer as she was leaving the house just a few hours ago. RETURN OF MISSING HEIRESS BRIDE! the headline blared at her, and underneath was a great deal of conjecture but few genuine facts.

When they reached the house she ducked down in her seat as the driver spoke into the intercom at the gate, but thankfully the press seemed to have called it a day.

Milo let her in, his eyes running over her, but he didn't ask where she'd been, simply saying, 'Have you eaten?' And when she said yes he went into the sitting-room at the back of the house where he was watching a programme on television.

Following him, Paige showed him the paper. 'I shouldn't have gone out while they were there,' she said ruefully. 'But maybe now they've got a picture they'll be satisfied and leave us alone.'

'I doubt it.' Milo pointed to a small pile of messages torn from the pad by the phone. 'Several papers have called, offering to buy our story.'

'What did you tell them?' she asked, going over to pick them up.

'That I don't approve of cheque-book journalism.'

Paige read one of the slips and whistled. 'Wow! Are they really willing to pay that much?'

'So they said.' Milo's eyes shifted from the television set to watch her.

She read through the slips, a look of amazement on her face, then dropped the lot in the waste-paper basket. 'Have you had dinner?' she asked.

'Mmm. I made myself an omelette.'

'You didn't wait for me, then?'

The programme came to an end and he switched off the set with the remote control. 'I wasn't sure that you'd be back,' he told her.

Immediately the tension was back between them, and Paige just wasn't in the mood. 'I'm going up to my room to phone Jean-Louis,' she told him. 'Goodnight.'

But when she rang the château in France she was told that everyone had gone out to dinner, so she didn't even have the consolation of talking to her fiancé. Would he care that Milo claimed they'd been lovers? she wondered. Probably not, but in any case she had no intention of telling him. She had no wish to test Jean-Louis's feelings for her by trying to make him jealous.

Feeling restless and not at all sleepy, Paige took a leisurely bath and then sat propped up in bed, glancing through a fashion magazine. But even the fact that she could now afford any of the gorgeous outfits it illustrated wasn't enough to hold her attention. She was listening for Milo to come upstairs, knowing that he would have to pass her bedroom to reach his own. And, this being an ordinary house rather than a hotel, there was no lock on the door.

The house was very quiet and she had to strain to hear anything, but at last heard a door close downstairs and then the soft tread of footsteps coming up the carpeted staircase. There was the click of a light switch and then the creak of an old floorboard as the steps came along the corridor towards her room. Paige gazed down at the open magazine on her lap, but she had become very still, all her senses alert, like a wild animal that scented danger might be near. Would he come in? Did he think that by telling her they had been lovers he now had the right to claim her again?

The footsteps slowed, came to a halt outside her door. Paige froze, fully aware that they were alone in the house and that there were no neighbours near enough to hear her if she cried out for help. But then the footsteps moved on and she slowly relaxed, letting out her held breath in a long, relieved sigh.

Something woke Paige early the next morning and she couldn't get to sleep again, even though she didn't seem to have slept much. She decided to try out the pool in the basement, putting on a new swimsuit that she'd bought and pulling a robe over it. Carefully she turned the knob of her door, not wanting to wake Milo, and ran lightly down the stairs, but found that the lights in the basement were already on. Paige slowed, moving cautiously forward in the shadow of one of the round, tiled pillars that divided the pool from the sauna and solarium. She could hear a faint splashing sound and when she peeped round the pillar she saw that Milo was there before her.

He was a strong swimmer, cutting through the water in a clean crawl and turning at each end with a lithe, graceful movement. He was also naked. Paige knew that she ought to get the hell out of there, but the glimpses of his tanned, athletic body as he cut through the water completely fascinated her. Taking advantage of the foliage of a large indoor plant close to the pillar, she drew back and watched him. After a while, Milo came to the far end of the pool and hauled himself out. He stood there for a moment with his back to her, then walked over to a towel that lay draped across a chair.

Picking it up, he began to dry himself the way men did, holding the towel by each end and rubbing it briskly across his back, and then down to his waist, his legs braced to keep his balance. His actions were so natural, and his body so beautiful, that Paige was unable to tear her eyes away. But why was the sight of him so disturbing when he'd told her they'd been lovers? She would have seen him naked before, would have felt his skin against her own, would have known the erotic pleasure that his hard body could give. Her skin felt on fire, and she could almost hear the beating of her heart, the uneven sigh of her breath.

Milo turned, and Paige hurriedly stepped back then ran through the house to her room. Still oddly agitated, she peeled off the swimsuit and dressed in ordinary clothes.

Half an hour later Milo found her in the kitchen, and she greeted him with a cool smile. 'I thought I'd fix breakfast this morning. Scrambled eggs OK?'

'That would be fine. Thank you.'

Sitting down at the table, he watched her as Paige busied herself with a saucepan. She glanced at him, then said, 'Don't you read the papers or something on Sunday mornings?'

'Don't you like being watched?'

'Cooking scrambled eggs the way they ought to be cooked—the French way—requires concentration,' she informed him. 'No distractions allowed.'

'And do I distract you?'

Paige remembered him naked and her voice wasn't quite steady as she said, 'Yes.'

She half expected him to follow up on that admission, but he merely said, 'In that case I'll collect the paper; I'd hate to spoil your culinary expertise.'

He didn't come back into the kitchen until she called him, and while they ate she said, 'Do you know what I'd like to do today?'

'The shops are closed. This is superb, by the way.'

'Good. No, I don't want to shop. Do you remember you promised to take me to the Caine and Chandos building? I'd like to go there.'

'None of the staff will be there on a Sunday,' Milo pointed out.

'I know. That's why I'd like to go today, without anyone staring at me.'

He gave her a contemplative look, then nodded. 'All right. We'll go this morning.'

The office building was in the City, near Farringdon Street, in one of the old Georgian blocks that had managed to survive not only the Blitz but also modern redevelopment. The floors were of marble, making their footsteps echo along the empty corridors, and the walls were mostly of panelled wood. Paige had half expected the offices to be equally dated, but instead found that they were fitted up with state-of-the-art technology, every desk having its own computer and bank of phones.

'We deal with foreign markets a lot,' Milo explained. 'And we need to be in constant touch with our customers and contacts.'

'Is the company expanding?'

'Yes, very much so. We've been lucky enough to be in a position to take advantage of companies that have gone under because of the world recession. Bad luck for them, of course.'

Or bad management, Paige thought. Somehow she couldn't imagine Milo ever being a loser—at least not where business was concerned. But with personal relationships, at least with his past relationship with her, it would seem he wasn't so successful.

They climbed the broad wooden staircase within the building and came to the executive offices on the third floor. Milo showed her his own office, the door simply marked 'Caine'—or rather suite of offices, because, besides what was obviously his busy working office, there was also a room that was more like a lounge, with settees set round a low coffee-table, a bar and a dining area. For entertaining clients, he told her. Next to that was the boardroom, a beautiful room with contemporary furniture—a huge oval table and chairs—set under a central crystal chandelier, the walls hung with portraits of past members of both families.

They went back through his office, but Milo hesitated, then said, 'Maybe this is a good moment to give you something that rightly belongs to you.'

He went over to a picture on the wall, a golden-framed landscape that to Paige, who had been to Giverny, shouted Monet.

'Is that an original?' she breathed.

Milo looked surprised. 'Yes, of course.' But he was sliding the picture to one side to reveal a wall-safe. After he'd pressed in some numbers the door swung open and he took out a small jeweller's box. Turning, he held it in his hand and flicked it open.

The ring inside the box was breathtaking, a huge rose-cut solitaire diamond that must have cost the earth. Paige's eyes flickered, then slowly lifted to gaze at the man she'd been engaged to. A question was large in her eyes but she didn't ask it. It was Milo who finally broke the silence by saying, 'It's your engagement ring.'

'It's very—beautiful.' She glanced down at her left hand on which she wore the ring that Jean-Louis had bought for her in a Paris antique shop. It too had diamonds, but they were very small ones that surrounded an opal. 'But this is my engagement ring now.'

'Of course,' Milo said smoothly. 'But this still belongs to you.'

'How did you get it? Did I give it back to you?'

He gave a twisted smile. 'There was no big scene when you flung it back in my face, if that's what you're thinking. It was found in the glove compartment of your car. When it was found the police gave everything it contained to your grandmother, and she passed it on to me.'

'She did the right thing,' Paige said quickly, her left hand creeping behind her back. 'It should belong to you. Thank you, but I'd rather you kept it.'

Milo slid it onto the little finger of his left hand but it only went up to the first joint. 'Somehow I don't think it would suit me,' he said with irony.

Smiling a little, she took it off his finger and replaced it in the padded velvet of the box, then walked over and put the box back in the safe. 'Maybe one day you'll find a use for it,' she said lightly.

'In what way?' His voice was cool.

She shrugged. 'I don't know.'

Curtly he said, 'There's no way I would ever give a ring that I bought for you, to mark your promise to marry me, to some other woman.'

'I didn't mean that.'

'Didn't you?'

'No!' She was annoyed herself now. 'Why don't you just take it back to the shop? Sell it? Give it to charity, or something? It's yours, not mine. Maybe it never was mine.'

'I've told you it was. And you saw it in the photographs I showed you in Paris,' he said stiffly.

'That wasn't what I meant.' She shook her head helplessly. 'Maybe wearing it never felt right.' Milo frowned, was about to speak, but she turned away. 'Show me the rest of the building.'

She walked out of the office, and after a moment Milo followed her.

On the other side of the boardroom was another office door, this one with a name-plate bearing the word 'Chandos'.

'This was your grandfather's office,' he told her.

Inside there was a different world. The room was exactly as it had been on the day her grandfather had used it for the last time, a few days before he died. Nothing had been changed. There was no computer, no digital phone or fax machine, just a big old partner's desk in rich mahogany, the leather top scratched and ink-stained from all the thousands of letters that had been written on its surface. On the desk were two photographs, both of young, beautiful women. One was in black and white, the woman with her hair up in a style that had been fashionable just after the war, and Paige saw with surprise that it was her grandmother. The other was a coloured photo of a girl with blonde hair not unlike her own.

'Your mother,' Milo said from behind her.

Slowly Paige put down the picture. 'Why have you never modernised this office?' she asked.

'We're waiting for the next member of the Chandos family to come along and take possession of it,' he said lightly.

'But there never will be one, will there? Not now.' She was suddenly and irrationally angry. 'Keeping this office like some mausoleum is ridiculous. You should make better use of it. Give it to one of the other directors. Or even turn it into a rest-room for the female office staff,' she added sardonically. 'Somewhere they can go and pull all the men to pieces.'

Milo's brows rose. 'Why so vehement?'

Paige looked at him for a moment, but then she shook her head and shrugged. 'I don't know. There's something about this room. I—I feel uneasy here.'

His mouth twisted. 'It was in this room that I first kissed you.'

'Oh.' For a moment she was astonished, but then laughed derisively and said, 'What a place to choose! And how did I react?'

To her annoyance Milo gave a reminiscent smile. 'Very satisfactorily.'

Paige gave him a sour look. 'I expect you took me by surprise.'

'No, I was the one who was surprised—by the response I got.' His hands were in his pockets but he moved nearer as he said, 'I expected a schoolgirl reaction—you know, all blushes and embarrassment. Either giggles or else tongue-tied shyness.' Standing very close, looking down at her, still with that smile playing on his lips, he added softly, 'But what I got was very different.'

With some misgivings, Paige said, 'Really?'

'Yes.' He moved closer still and she backed away but was trapped against the desk. 'You were very responsive, very—eager.'

Her throat dry, Paige said, 'I can't think why.'

'Can't you?' His legs, his body were touching hers, not pressing hard but so close that she could feel the heat of him. 'Because you were longing for me to kiss you, of course. Because it was what you wanted.' His eyes were holding her gaze, daring her to look away. Paige was aware that he still had his hands in his pockets, so it must have been the desire in his eyes that made her feel as if he was caressing her, as if every nerve end was on fire with an urgent need to be touched and explored. It would have been so easy to reach up and put her arms round his neck, to experience again the kiss he had given her the other night.

And what would he do then? Lay her back on the desk and take her? Make love to her until her cries awakened the ghosts that haunted this old room? Hastily she lowered her eyes, not wanting him to see the wantonness of her thoughts. He was talking of another and very important kiss, one given and taken willingly, but with emotions that no longer existed. His breath was warm against her neck as he said softly, 'Don't you remember it, Paige? Can't you remember how good it was?'

'No!' Pushing him roughly aside, she stepped out of the circle of sensuality he had created, the word more a repudiation of the emotions he had evoked in her than a denial of the memory he was trying to bring back to her mind. The distance between them making her calmer, she said, 'No, I don't remember—and I don't want to. What was between us in the past—and it doesn't seem to have gone very deep—is over. Finished.'

'You're wrong when you say it didn't go deep.' His hands were out of his pockets now and Milo's voice had become forceful. 'You insult us both when you disparage what we felt for each other.'

She was about to make a sharp retort, but there was something in his eyes, a raw bleakness, that made her pause, and after a moment she said stiffly, 'I'm sorry. But you don't seem to understand how difficult all this is for me. You want to go back to how it was in the past, but I can't do that. I'm not the same person that you knew. Surely you can see that?'

'Oh, I agree that you seem to be different. But it's all superficial. No one can change their personality so completely in just a year. You're still the same basic person that you were, and I'm sure that deep down your feelings are still the same, too.'

'You seem to forget that all I feel for you is hate,' she pointed out sharply.

'I don't buy that.' He moved towards her again. 'And, anyway, love and hate are very close emotions.'

Paige moved away, snapped out, 'Stop doing this!'

'Doing what?'

'You know damn well what. You're trying to—to coerce me.'

'Maybe you want to be coerced.'

'You must be joking!'

'Maybe you *want* to feel all the emotions you felt before—all the need, the longing, all the love.'

His voice was insinuating, persuasive, but Paige wasn't going to fall for that one. 'Look, I've been willing to tolerate you and your—your behaviour because right now I'm alone and I need you. But if you touch me again, if you even come close, then I'm leaving. I mean it! I'm in love with another man and I'm going to marry him. I'll stay at your house only so long as you agree that our—our relationship is on a strictly business footing. And if you can't handle that then you'd better say so now. Because there's no way I'll ever be interested in you, and nothing you say or do will change that. Do you understand?'

Again his face became an enigmatic mask. 'Oh, yes, I understand.'

'And do you agree to those terms?'

'It would seem I have no choice.'

'No, you don't. Good.' Quickly she stepped to the door and pulled it open. 'Let's move on.'

A look of disappointment came into his eyes, and it was obvious that Milo had hoped that evoking what, for him, were poignant memories might also bring something of the past back to her. But Paige walked determinedly away from it, as determinedly as she had run out on him before.

But as he continued to show her over the building, and again after they'd had lunch and were walking through Hyde Park, Paige wondered whether there had been some truth in his observation. Did she subconsciously want to go back into the past? She supposed she needn't have come back to England with him; if she had really been dead-set against it then neither Milo nor Jean-Louis—nothing on earth— could have persuaded her. Yet she had come, super- ficially to claim her inheritance, but perhaps drawn by feelings so deep that she could hardly recognise them, let alone define them. Although it had, of course, been pure chance that Milo had seen her portrait, and that Jean-Louis had painted it in the first place. She'd been so reluctant to sit for him, she remembered, but he had kept on and on at her until finally she had given in.

It occurred to Paige that she'd read somewhere that nothing was coincidental, that everything was meant. Maybe that was why she had finally given in to Jean-Louis and let him paint her portrait: had she, deep in her subconscious, known that she had a past, known that Milo might see the picture and come for her? That thought made her feel extremely uneasy and she pushed it aside, concentrated on being cool and aloof.

When they left and were driving back to Hampstead, Milo fished in his pocket and handed her a card. 'I've made an appointment for you to see this man tomorrow afternoon.'

The card bore a name with a whole string of letters after it, and an address in Harley Street. Paige had never heard of the man but immediately guessed that he must be some kind of doctor. Stiffly she said, 'Who is he?'

'He specialises in cases like yours. People who're suffering from amnesia.'

She gave him a fierce, angry glare. 'I am not a case!'

'He might be able to help you get your memory back.'

Paige's face tightened and her knuckles showed white as she gripped the card, but then she laughed derisively. 'And do you really think I want it back? Do you seriously think that I want to remember the life I had with my grandmother? Or my—relationship with you?' Lifting the card so that he could see, she deliberately tore it in half. 'If and when I decide that my past life was so wonderful that I just have to know about it, then *I'll* make my own appointment to see a shrink.'

'He isn't a shrink. He's a—'

'I don't give a damn what he is! You had no right to make the appointment. You are not my keeper. You are *nothing* to me.' Her hands shaking, she dropped the pieces of paper on the floor, then turned and concentrated on looking out of the window.

Milo glanced at her averted head for a moment, his face grim, then he, too, looked away and concentrated on his driving.

The next day Paige got up to find herself alone with Milo's housekeeper, Eileen, a buxom, middle-aged and very capable woman, who informed her that Milo had already left for his office. 'He always leaves early; a workaholic, he is,' Eileen told her, relishing the word.

It seemed she had never met Paige before, having started working for Milo only six months ago, although she obviously knew all about her and was filled with curiosity. But Milo must have told her not to ask questions, so she didn't—not directly—although she came out with some very inviting remarks that begged Paige to confide in her. It was an invitation Paige resisted with a smile, soon leaving the house to go and see Charles Readman.

The solicitor told her that her fingerprints had proved her identity, and he proceeded to give her an inventory of everything she owned. There was no real estate apart from the house in Chelsea, which she instructed him to put on the market, any property her parents had owned in England having been sold and the proceeds divided between them when they had divorced. But there was a large portfolio of stocks and shares as well as her shares in Caine and Chandos. In fact she was, as Milo had told her back in Paris, quite a rich woman. And, as Charles Readman pointed out, she was also her grandmother's only heir; when old Mrs Chandos died she would be very rich indeed.

Paige found that idea completely unpalatable, but comforted herself with the thought that she and her grandmother had parted on such bad terms that the old lady was far more likely to leave her money to a cats' home than to her. But, even so, she had enough in her own right to keep Jean-Louis in Armani suits for the foreseeable future. She had to sign several documents, more because she was now over twenty-one and had come into her inheritance than because she had returned to England. But when she came out of his office she had been, officially at least, reinstated into her old character. She was Paige Chandos, and Angélique Castet was once more nothing but a name and a date written on a scrap of paper that had been found in her pocket.

It was almost frightening how easily she had slipped back into this life, like putting on an old coat that was warm and comfortable. But Paige didn't want that; Milo was wrong and she *was* different, had changed completely. She was convinced of that, of course, but still had a hunted feeling that she ought to get back to Jean-Louis as quickly as possible.

Over the next week or so she talked to him often on the phone, but somehow the conversations were never satisfactory; he always seemed to be busy or on the point of going out, and he complained one evening that the American woman wanted to get back to the States. 'But I refuse to hurry my work,' Jean-Louis told her. 'If necessary I will go with her to California and finish the picture there. In fact, that might be a good idea. I will probably collect many commissions in America. Unless you save me by claiming your inheritance.' Then he added impatiently, as he always did, 'Has it been settled yet?'

'Not completely,' Paige prevaricated, annoyed at being coerced. It seemed that both men were tugging at her, trying to make her do what they wanted. But to hell with them both, she thought angrily; she'd belong only to herself for a while. And it was pleasant to be in London with money to spend and so many places to go.

After her ultimatum Milo had behaved with careful correctness but had invited her to go with him to an art exhibition. Bored by being on her own, she had agreed, and that had led to tickets for the ballet, an antique fair, a box at the opera. And she had to admit that being escorted by Milo wasn't exactly unpleasant—so long as he behaved himself, of course. He did, but that didn't prevent tension rising between them, caused, as much as anything, by his stiff courtesy as he kept his word not to touch her. It didn't make for easy living, and Paige often found herself too uptight to relax at night.

To relieve the tension, she got into the habit of going down to the sauna for half an hour before going to bed every night, lying on the padded massage table in the middle of the small room as she let the stresses of the day evaporate with the heat. One night the sauna was so soporific that she fell deeply asleep, face down on her folded arms, and didn't hear the door open some time later. It was only when she felt Milo's hands on her bare shoulders that she came to with a start.

'Hey!' she exclaimed.

But he said soothingly, 'Lie still.' His hands went

to her neck, felt the knots of tension there, and he began gently to stroke his thumbs down her nape. 'You were fast asleep.'

She tried to get up. 'I told you not to touch me.'

But he held her down, saying, 'I'm not—not the way you mean. This is completely impersonal. Why were you asleep?'

'Because I was tired, presumably,' she said sardonically.

'Don't you sleep at night?'

Paige hesitated, then said, 'Not very well, no.'

'Is your bed uncomfortable?'

'No, it's fine.' He had put some oil on his hands and was running his thumbs down her neck in long strokes that gradually got to her.

'So maybe you're finding it difficult to sleep for the same reason I am.'

'Oh?' she said guardedly.

'Yes. Knowing you're so close, knowing we're alone in the house, and wanting you so much, doesn't make for a relaxing night.'

She gasped, but said at once, 'If you think I feel any of those things you're crazy.'

Milo laughed softly. 'You know, Paige, you really shouldn't try and tell lies when someone is giving you a massage; your neck has suddenly gone rigid. You'll give yourself away every time.'

'I just don't trust you, that's all. And I want you to stop.'

'Of course, when you're relaxed,' he said calmly.

Paige thought of pushing him away, but she was bare except for a towel wrapped round her middle and was afraid of losing it. So she stayed still and thought how expert his hands were, how firm and yet gentle

at the same time. 'Where did you learn to do this?'
she asked after a while.

'I had some sports training years ago.'

He had put on more oil and his hands were working
on her shoulders and upper arms now, warm and
soothing. Paige closed her eyes, letting the sensation
of being pampered take over. Soon she would tell him
that she'd had enough, make him go away so that she
could shower, then put on her robe and go up to bed.
But she was so warm and comfortable; there was time
enough. Moving down the table, Milo began to massage her legs, starting at her feet. Paige laughed, said,
'Hey, I'm ticklish.'

There was amusement in Milo's voice as he said,
'Sorry. I'd forgotten.'

He ran a finger along the delicate sole of her foot,
making her squirm, but then lifted it so that he could
rub her toes, carefully doing each one before moving
up to her ankles. Paige relaxed again, and tried to
ignore the fact that she was loving this. Milo took his
time. When he'd massaged her feet to his satisfaction,
he worked on her calves, his hands skilful, the oil
mingling with the light perspiration on her skin. It
seemed very hot in the small room, hotter even than
the normal temperature, which was high enough. He
was working on the backs of her knees, his hands
brushing against the bottom of her towel. Her eyes
were shut but she was very aware of his touch, of the
trails of heat his hands left behind. But it wouldn't go
on for much longer; he had massaged both her legs
and her shoulders now, and she waited for him to
stand back and tell her he was done.

But with a quick and totally unexpected movement
he parted the towel so that she was revealed to his
gaze. Paige gave a cry of protest, but already his

hands were on her upper legs where he'd left off, and he was saying, 'Relax. You'd let a professional masseur do this, wouldn't you? So where's the difference?'

'There's a hell of a difference, and you know it.' She tried to cover herself again but it was impossible when she was lying on her front, and she had no intention of turning over.

'Don't you like it?' He was working on her back again, leaning over her, concentrating on what he was doing.

'No.'

Milo laughed in disbelief and stroked his hands down her sides, his fingers just touching her breasts. The oil he was using was aromatic, the herbs it contained filling the air, strong, musky and sensuous. Fully awake now, Paige was aware of every nerve-end, of the eroticism of his touch, of the growing sensations of concupiscence deep inside her. She tried to ignore them, but his hands wouldn't let her; they continually sought and found new areas to excite as he moved on down to her waist and then to her hips and thighs.

She could hear his breath, deep and unsteady as he worked, sometimes felt his bare arm as he moved it across her when he reached for more oil. But she didn't dare to look at him. Instead she lay very still now, her mouth dry, her heart thudding, her body on fire. He ran his hands all the way down from her neck to her feet and she was unable to resist a tremor of awareness, a tremor that gave way to a gasp, which became a stifled moan as he moved slowly up again but paused halfway to touch and explore gently.

'Paige.' His voice was soft but almost hoarse with

need as he leaned closer to her ear, his hands still caressing. 'Turn over, my darling.'

For a moment she didn't react, knowing what he wanted, knowing that if she did as he begged everything would change. If she gave herself to him now it would have to be a total commitment, her whole life, the future, everything. She lay very still, too paralysed to move, but then he touched her again and the shock of it went to her very soul. With a groan almost of despair, she slowly turned and lay naked before him. Then reached out for him.

CHAPTER SEVEN

SLOWLY, hardly daring to breathe in case he broke the spell, Milo leaned over and ran his hand gently down Paige's face. Her incredible eyes were huge green pools that were a strange, haunting mixture of both fear and desire. His lips trembling with the effort to control himself, he sought her mouth and tenderly kissed her. Her arms went round his neck and he felt the fire in her, recognised the hunger he had aroused.

His kiss changed completely then as he allowed his own overwhelming need to take over. He had intended to massage her front, to go on slowly rousing her until she was unable to resist, her inhibitions gone, but he saw that there was no need for that. Already her body was fully alive to the hands that caressed her, her nipples hard under his questing fingers and exploring mouth. She moaned as he touched her and arched towards him, kissed him fiercely when he found her mouth again for a brief moment before moving on to continue his tantalising exploration. Her breath raw and panting, Paige opened heavy-lidded eyes as she held his head against her while he kissed her, loving it but finding it a thrill so exciting that she could hardly bear it.

'Milo! Oh, God, Milo.' The words were a plea, an invitation, a demand.

Unable to control his harsh, panting breath, he raked his tongue across the soft swell of her stomach, collecting the tiny drops of moisture that clung to her skin, finding it the most perfect nectar, the honey of

133

life. She cried out, half sat up as she reached for him, the yearning deep inside her becoming a frenzy now. He came up onto the table and knelt between her feet. He was naked, had been all the time and she hadn't known. But now he let her see him, wanted her to. Wanted her to see how much he needed her. She stared, her eyes huge again, then let him bear her down until she lay under him.

He kissed her passionately, until she was lost again under the uncontrollable urgency for love. And he took her fiercely because he'd waited for so many unendurable months, not knowing there was any need for gentleness until she cried out, not in excitement, but in pain. For a moment she fought him, but it was too late and he couldn't stop, and then the pain was gone and it was all pleasure, pleasure, pleasure.

Their cries filled the little room, were softened by the wooden walls, became lost in the curling steam. It was the most wonderful and yet the strangest moment of Milo's life. He had wanted her for so long, had been tortured by the thought of her going with other men, and now to find that she was still a virgin! His mind was totally confused, but could only be infinitely grateful for such a miracle. He kissed her, groaned out her name as they clung to each other, and almost, it seemed, before they had finished making love the first time she was moving under him, refusing to let him go, and they were experiencing the wonder of it all over again.

Afterwards, Milo lay beside her, for the moment completely exhausted, but with a huge, contented grin on his face. He had his arm under her head as they lay side by side, and she could feel the hammering of his heart, hear his ragged breathing as he gradually recovered. When he could speak, he said, with gratified astonishment rather than rancour, 'You minx, you lied to me.'

Paige laughed, supremely confident in the new awareness of her own body and the pleasure it could give her—no, that Milo could give her. 'So, it seems, did you.'

'Mmm.' He kissed her shoulder. 'I'm sorry if I hurt you. If I'd known...'

'I'm glad you didn't. It was—' she looked at him with eyes that were both possessive and full of wonder '—it was so right. Perfect.'

'Oh, Paige.' He gathered her to him and kissed her deeply, then stroked aside the damp hair that clung to her forehead. 'I love you so much, so very much.'

Her eyes were misty but smiling as she touched his face before returning his kiss.

Softly he said, 'Why did you lie about Jean-Louis?'

But Paige put her fingers over his mouth. 'Hush. I don't want to talk. Not now. Not yet.'

'You're right. This is hardly the place.'

A shower cubicle opened off the sauna; Milo carried her in there and they stood very close together as the water cascaded over them. He used his hands to wash her, and they kissed again, oblivious to everything but the intoxication of sexual intimacy, of the knowledge that they now had of each other's body. At last Milo turned off the shower, found towels and bathrobes and carried her upstairs to his own room. Paige knew why when she saw the size of the fourposter there.

'Is this the *master* bed?' she gurgled when he laid her on it.

'Definitely.' He unwound the towel from round her head. 'Here, let me dry your hair for you.'

She sat up and he knelt behind her, gently rubbing

life back into the long golden strands. But after a few minutes her loose robe slipped from her shoulders and he could see her breasts. They looked so pert and delicious that he groaned. 'Do up your robe,' he ordered.

'Why?' Paige asked innocently, but knowing the reason full well.

'Because if you don't I shall have to take you again.'

'Really?' After a moment she looked at him over her shoulder. 'So what are you waiting for?'

'You witch,' he breathed. 'You beautiful, entrancing witch.' Reaching forward, he began to caress her breasts, but soon this wasn't enough and he slid alongside her to throw off her robe and make love to her again with a consummate skill that lifted Paige to new heights of dizzying pleasure before attaining his own tremendous climax.

Afterwards, her body still floating in a wonderful cloud of fulfilment, Paige said on a dreamy chuckle, 'Now this is a *mistress* bed, too.'

His voice hoarse and ragged, Milo said, 'Not on your life. You're going to be my *wife*.'

'Am I?' She smiled, her lids still closed. 'That sounds good to me.'

'It does?' He came up on his elbow and gazed down at her in astounded happiness.

She opened her beautiful eyes and looked at him. 'Yes, it does,' she assured him.

His voice choked with emotion, Milo said, 'I've—I've waited so long for you to say that. Despaired that it would never happen. Having come so close and then lost you—' He broke off, momentarily overcome, but then took her hand and raised it to his lips in overwhelming gratitude.

'It seems that we were always meant for each other, doesn't it?' she said huskily.

'Of course. It was inevitable. I've known it from the first moment I saw you.'

'Will we be married soon?'

'Very soon, my love.'

'And will we make love every night?'

Supremely happy, Milo was able to tease her a little. 'Do you want to?'

'Oh, definitely.'

He nibbled her ear. 'In that case we shall make love every night and every morning,' he vowed.

'In the mornings, too. Is that allowed?' she asked, stroking his chest.

'Only when you're married,' he assured her.

That made her laugh. But then she frowned and licked her lips. 'I'm so thirsty.'

'I'll get something to drink.' He lifted her hair, which had dried into a mass of curls, and kissed her throat. 'Don't go away.'

She chuckled. 'I may *never* leave this bed.'

When he came back she was almost asleep and he had to blow on her neck to rouse her. 'Hey, I thought you were thirsty.'

'Oh, I am.' Paige sat up, completely natural in her nakedness. 'Oh, champagne. Wonderful!'

'It's the only drink that's right for tonight,' Milo told her as he opened the bottle and caught the frothing wine in a pair of tall glasses. 'Here, my darling. To us—and to all the nights that will be as wonderful as tonight.'

'Oh, I'll drink to that.' Paige did so, drinking the bubbling liquid down thirstily.

Milo shook his head at her, and smilingly said,

'Didn't anyone ever tell you you're supposed to sip champagne, not toss it back like mineral water?'

'I promise to sip the next one,' she said, and held out the glass.

He had put on a robe to go down to the wine cellars, but now Milo shrugged it off as he took her glass to refill it.

Paige looked at him in fascination. His body was as lean and muscular as any athlete's, as straight and smooth and beautiful as Michelangelo's *David*. 'Your body is perfect,' she said with sincerity. 'I thought it was only statues of men that were beautiful; I didn't know that real men could be too.'

'Thank you.' He handed her the champagne and Paige leaned back against the bed-head as she drank it, her eyes still on him. 'But this isn't the first time you've seen me naked. What about a week or so ago when I was swimming in the pool and you watched me?'

With a delighted laugh, she said, 'I didn't think you'd seen me.'

'I didn't—but I just knew you were there. Maybe I'm psychic where you're concerned.'

She laughed richly again, and, half-asleep and more than a little light-headed from the champagne, from making love and from being proposed to, said without thinking, 'You always were. Do you remember that time I hid in the cupbo—?' She broke off, appalled. Milo's shoulders tensed and he swung his head round to look at her. Quickly she tried to cover it, adding hastily, 'When you came to Paris and—and found me. That—that was purely psychic.'

But her voice faded as she saw stunned realisation

come into his eyes. Reaching out, Milo caught her
wrist, holding her prisoner as mounting fury darkened
his face.

CHAPTER EIGHT

IT WAS Paige's eyes that had given her away. Those
incredible eyes that he loved so much and which had
been the means of him finding her again. They had
filled with not only horrified dismay but guilt. Looking into them, Milo had suddenly seen it all. It had
been like opening a book and reading there the answer
to all the questions that had tortured him for so long,
questions he had thought answered. But now he saw
that it had all been lies; the book had proved to be
nothing but fiction. In those few seconds his happiness, so precious and so newly regained, shattered in
his face all over again. It was like a physical blow,
so severe that his hand tightened convulsively on her
arm and he gave an involuntary sound that was part
groan of pain and part an overwhelming cry of anger
against the fates that had stabbed him in the heart yet
again.

And she had tried to brazen it out! She would have
gone on deceiving him if she could. That thought
filled him with fury, a rage so black he could hardly
see through it. He jerked her towards him so violently
that Paige's drink flew from her hand, the wine making an arc of liquid that for a fleeting instant caught
the light like a rainbow. Neither of them noticed it.
His face murderous, Milo glared down at her, glad
that there was alarm now in her eyes.

'You bitch!' he got out. 'You cruel, lying little
bitch!'

'No! No, you don't understand.' Although he

140

hadn't raised his hand against her, Paige put up her free arm as if to ward him off.

'Don't I?' His voice was ragged with anger. 'All right, you tell me, then. What don't I understand?'

The direct question took her aback, and Milo could almost see her mind racing, hear her thinking. Would she again try to brazen it out, try to convince him that he'd made a mistake? Or would she think up some excuse? Grimly he waited.

With a tentative smile Paige put her free hand up to her head. 'I—I remembered something, didn't I? Maybe my memory is starting to come back.'

His eyes filling with contempt, Milo said glacially, 'Or maybe you've been lying the whole time and you never lost it. That's the real truth, isn't it? Is this some sort of perverted game? Is there nothing that means anything to you?'

She looked at him steadily, her beautiful eyes pools of assurance and tenderness. 'Yes,' Paige said huskily. 'My love for you means everything to me. It always—'

'Liar!' He yelled the word at her. 'I'm sick of your lies. I want the truth, do you hear me?' He shouted the words at her, shaking her as he did so. 'It was a lie, wasn't it? It was all a lie. You never lost your memory.'

He shook her so hard that she couldn't answer him. Paige put up her arms to try to push him away but her strength was that of a kitten against a lion. She gave a sob, her teeth rattling, then suddenly screamed out, 'All right! I did pretend. But—'

Milo stopped shaking her so abruptly that she fell against him. For a moment they were chest to chest and he felt the full softness of her breasts pressed against him. Her physical closeness brought back their lovemaking like an explosion, but the thought of having had sex with her and the knowledge of how badly he had wanted her made him suddenly feel sick to his stomach. Pushing her roughly away, he grabbed her robe and threw it to her. 'Put this on,' he snarled.

Striding over to his own clothes, he pulled them on anyhow, standing with his back to her, not wanting to look at her. Only when he was dressed again did he turn round. Paige had put on the robe and was standing at the other side of the bed. Her face was very white, almost as pale as the whiteness of the robe, and her eyes were huge, vulnerable and afraid. When she saw him turn towards her she gave another sob and ran round the bed to him, caught his arm and looked up at him pleadingly. 'Milo, please listen to me. I can explain…'

He shook her off, said with cold ferocity, 'Good—because that's what I want—an explanation.' Striding to the far side of the room, as far away from her as it was possible to get, he leaned against the wall, folded his arms and waited.

She put her hands up to her face, covering her mouth as she tried to get her breath back and control her voice, but it was still shaking, and Paige bit her lip a couple of times before she said, 'I did lose my memory when I was in France. I swear it!' she added forcefully when she saw his lips curl in disbelief. 'But when you brought me back here, when I saw the flat, and then—' her hands balled into fists '—and then you kissed me that first time…things began to come back. Not all at once; there wasn't some great revelation. Some things are still a blank. But with every day that went by I began to remember more.'

'But you didn't see fit to tell me,' Milo said with infinite sarcasm. 'Maybe you didn't think I'd be interested. Or did it just amuse you to go on pretending, to go on letting me suffer agonies, wondering if I'd ever get you back, whether I'd lost you for good?'

She made a begging motion with her hands and said earnestly, 'I know you won't believe me but I—I did it for you. I really did.'

He laughed, the jarring sound harsh and full of bitterness. 'You're right, I don't believe you.'

'I didn't want to hurt you,' she flung at him, deep distress in her face and tears in her eyes.

If her performance was designed to move him, to make him feel sorry for her, it failed completely. She had lied to him, and he was only just beginning to feel how deep the pain had gone. 'Am I supposed to be grateful?' he asked with harsh sarcasm.

Her head came up. 'Yes!' She flung the word at him, but then bit her lip again and hung her head, shaking it. 'No, I suppose that's impossible.'

'You're damn right it is.' He wanted to hurt her—physically, mentally, in any way he could—and he had to keep his arms tightly folded, his fists clenched, to stop himself grabbing her and shaking her again.

Pushing her hair back from her face, Paige wiped away a tear at the same time, then took a couple of breaths before saying in an unsteady, husky voice, 'When you found me in Paris and I saw those photos, I felt so frightened, so threatened. I knew instinctively that there had been something between us, but I couldn't remember anything. There were no facts, only terribly confused feelings, but such *strong* feelings. Anger, hatred. Then you said that I'd run away from you, which made me even more afraid.' Her words had become disjointed, heavy with tears. But she seemed to be making a huge effort to control herself.

Milo waited, watching her cynically, wondering why he'd never realised before what a brilliant actress she was.

'When my memory started to come back,' she went on after a few moments, 'I realised how much I'd loved you before, and how much I longed for everything to come right between us again now—' Paige broke off as Milo gave a sound of utter disbelief. Her mouth tightening, she somehow carried on, saying, 'But the past was such a mess. I'd been angry and humiliated enough to run away, and you must have hated me for what I'd put you through. I thought how wonderful it would be if we could just begin all over again with a clean slate. Then it occurred to me that in a way we had started again, and that maybe we could go on getting to know one another afresh. But we could only do that if my memory stayed lost, if the past didn't interfere. So if I pretended that my memory hadn't come back then maybe—perhaps— this time things might work out for us. And they had worked out.' Her voice rallied a little. 'Everything was wonderful until…'

'Until I found out that you're a liar and a cheat,' he finished for her. 'I don't believe a word of this. None of it! I think you were only using amnesia as an excuse. I think you just like playing with a man's deepest emotions—not once but twice! Who makes promises she has no intention of keeping. Who enjoys lifting a man to the heights of happiness and then plunging him down to the depths of despair.

'What would you have done if I hadn't found out?' he jeered. 'Arranged another wedding and then walked out on me again at the last minute to go back to Jean-Louis?' His jaw locked as he strove to control the most agonising bleakness. His feelings seemed to be coming in waves, one moment intense anger, the next a crashing sense of loss and unhappiness. Emotions that had once been all too familiar and were now again to fill his future. His voice raw, unnatural, he said fiercely, *'What the hell did I do to you to make you so damn vindictive?'*

'I didn't set out to be. I was desperate! I just had to get away, be my own person for a while. I was so unsure of myself. And my grandmother kept pushing me. It wasn't you—at least not entirely. I…' She gave an expressive, helpless shrug. 'If I hadn't run away, if I'd gone ahead with the wedding the way everybody wanted, I would have made you terribly unhappy.'

Milo gave a scornful, incredulous laugh. 'So that's the way you've explained it to yourself, is it? You did me a big favour by running away so that *I* wouldn't be unhappy? Well, thanks a million.'

'It's true! OK, you can't see it now. But when you've cooled off—'

'Don't count on it,' Milo interrupted nastily.

Paige's shoulders straightened, but slowly, as if carrying a great load. 'You're angry, and you have every right to be. But wasn't it easier for you to go on believing that I'd lost my memory? Wasn't it more—more comfortable for you to have everyone believing that?'

'Oh, I see, it was just a sop to my pride, was it? How *immensely* kind of you.'

'I was thinking of you,' she protested.

His face changed, grew murderous. 'And were you thinking of me when you ran away in the first place? Did it never occur to you that if you really cared about my feelings you would have discussed all your problems, asked me to give you some time, not just disappeared off the face of the earth?'

'But you wouldn't have,' she said simply. 'You kept pushing forward the wedding, and Grandmother kept pushing me to marry you. But I'd heard rumours about you—and then I got the letter and saw you with that woman.' Anger suddenly came into her voice. 'What the hell was I supposed to think? It was all too rushed, too convenient for you. I didn't know whether or not I could trust you. And you never—' She gulped. 'You were never eager, loving. You didn't attempt to make love to me, take me to bed.'

Milo gasped in astounded anger. 'I respected your innocence,' he thundered at her.

'I didn't want my innocence respected. How could you be so blind? I wanted you to be so eager to make love to me that you couldn't wait. I wanted you to *need* me, to be crazy for me.' She gave an abrupt gesture with her hand. 'Can you imagine what it was like for me? I'd been rejected by both my parents and handed over to my grandmother, a woman who was incapable of showing even affection, let alone love. I thought it was my fault. I thought that I wasn't a lovable person. Then I met you and I really fell for you. You seemed so perfect, so wonderful. It was like a miracle when you proposed to me. But you were always so distant. That time in my grandfather's office when we kissed for the first time—you seemed amused because I'd put my heart and soul into kissing you. It made me feel stupid, inhibited.' Paige looked at Milo expectantly, but his face was a cold, grim mask and he didn't speak.

She shivered and rubbed her arms as if his look had turned her to ice. 'Then I heard the rumours about you only wanting me so that you could get complete control of the company. You said it wasn't so, that you loved me, but every time I tried to—to arouse you you just held me off, said we'd wait till the wedding. And then I found out about your mistress.'

'So you took the coward's way out and just disappeared,' Milo sneered, far too bitter and angry to be moved by what he'd heard.

'Yes, all right, if you like. Or maybe I just wanted to give myself a breathing space, to sort out my feelings. I decided to go to France, to try to find my father's relatives. That's why I had Angélique Castet's details in my pocket; I'd got them from a church record. My bag, with all my papers inside, was destroyed in the fire when the bus crashed. And when I came round in the hospital the people there called me Angélique, so I thought that was who I was. I spoke the language and I thought I was French. It was a terribly confusing time. I had to build a new life from the beginning. Learn to take care of myself. Make new friends. Maybe even find someone who really wanted and needed me,' she retorted.

He laughed disdainfully. 'And you ended up with Jean-Louis.'

'Yes. But Jean-Louis cared about me—and he certainly wanted me.' She gave a sad, hollow laugh. 'But I realise now that I did to him what you did to me—I held out and made him wait.' She frowned as she thought about it. 'Perhaps there was always the knowledge of you deep down in my subconscious, holding me back. I don't know. But there was always something that made me say no to him. Maybe in my heart I was hoping that you would find me.' She shook her head, hands at her temples. 'I just don't know. When Jean-Louis asked me to marry him I held out for a long time, but then we got engaged and I might have gone ahead and married him. But I let him paint the portrait—and then you came.'

'I wish I'd never seen it,' Milo said forcefully, and certainly meaning it.

But pride came into Paige's lifted head as she said, 'That isn't true. You're just lying to yourself. Because my plan worked. We did start afresh. And this time you certainly wanted me. You couldn't wait to make love to me. And it was right and wonderful. You can't possibly deny that.'

But Milo was still so embittered, felt so cheated, that it was impossible for him to see past his own feelings. All the old emotions of a year ago had come flooding back, but increased a hundredfold. Right now he hated the very sight of her. He felt that he had been taken in, duped, humiliated, and he couldn't forgive her for that. To hurt her, he said, 'Yes, I wanted you—who wouldn't want a woman who flaunted herself the way you do? You advertised it for sale, could hardly wait to give it away. So I took you—so what?'

Paige flushed, bright spots of colour in her still pale cheeks. 'That was cheap and nasty.'

'Really? Just like you, then.'

That made her angry and she cried out, 'I am not cheap!'

'No?' Again he deliberately hurt her. 'But it was hardly a cultural penetration.'

'You swine!'

Goaded, she took a furious stride towards him, raising her hand to hit him, but Milo caught her wrist. For a couple of minutes he held her like that, but she was too close and he could smell her perfume, feel her body against his. Suddenly afraid of how his own body might react, he abruptly pushed her away. But he had left it a few seconds too long and she had seen the fleeting panic in his eyes. A flicker of something that could have been hope or triumph came into her face and Milo hated her even more for it, and himself for having shown the slightest weakness.

Straightening up, he said, 'Get out of this room. And I want you out of the house first thing in the morning.'

To his astonishment she faced up to him and said clearly, 'No, I don't think so.'

'What the hell is that supposed to mean?'

'I won't leave. You invited me here and I'm staying.'

He gave an incredulous laugh. 'Like hell you are! You're going if I have to throw you out in the street with my own hands.'

But a mutinous look came into her green eyes and she said maliciously, 'That should look good in the papers.'

'Don't try to blackmail me because it won't work. I never want to see you again, let alone live under the same roof as you. You're going.'

'What time?'

'What?'

'What time are you going to throw me out? I'd like to know so that I can tell the press photographers what time to get here.'

Milo clenched his fists. Never in his life had he even been tempted to hit a woman, but it was taking every ounce of control he had not to do so now. 'All right,' he said, goaded almost beyond endurance. 'Stay, then. *I'll* leave.'

'I'll find out where you are. I'll follow you. I'll come to the office and make a scene. Is that really what you want?'

'What's the matter?' he said curtly. 'Haven't you

finished punishing me for the dreadful crime of actually loving you and wanting to marry you? Are you going to go on with it for the rest of your life?'

'I am *not* trying to punish you!' Her voice was fervent, entreating. 'You're punishing yourself.'

'Oh, sure. I'm having a great time opening up old wounds and twisting the knife in them.' Immediately he had said it, Milo was angry with himself, fearing the self-pitying image it might create. To counteract it, he immediately attacked. 'Just what do you hope to gain by staying here, by staying in my life? We're through, finished. I'm fed up to the teeth with the act you're putting on. I don't believe anything you say any more. I think you're just a vindictive little tart who wants to get her own back because things didn't work out the way you wanted them. I think you enjoy playing with men's emotions, having power over them. And I think—'

'But I *gave* myself to you.' She suddenly broke in on him, yelling the words out. 'If I was only playing cat and mouse with you would I have done that?'

'Oh, so you did. Am I supposed to be so grateful that I'll forgive you for everything else? Is that why you did it—to keep me besotted in case I found out the truth?'

'I was going to tell you. I meant to—'

His laugh of utter disbelief made her break off.

Paige tilted her head back, her throat taut as she fought to control herself. Her voice lower but unsteady, she said, 'I didn't tell you my memory had come back because I love you. I've always loved you. And I believe, I truly believe now, that you love me too. And I'm not going to let you throw that away. I don't care how angry you get or how much you try to humiliate me. I'm staying with you and I'm going to make you admit that you care about me.'

Watching her cynically, Milo could almost admire the act she was putting on. Lifting his hands, he gave her a slow clap. 'Bravo! A bravura performance,' he sneered. 'You really should be on the stage: you'd wow the audience. But unfortunately it doesn't do a thing for me.' He glared at her. 'I don't want you. Not now, not ever. So why don't you just run back to Jean-Louis and jump into bed with him? I'm sure he'd be a willing victim to your sadistic little games and—'

This time her hand flew at him without warning and he had to jerk backwards to avoid the stinging slap she'd aimed at his face. But then she was raining blows at him with her clenched fists, trying to hurt, smouldering anger in her eyes. He tried to catch her wrists but she was hitting at him so wildly that she got in several punches before he overpowered her.

'You're crazy!' Swinging her up, he put her over his shoulder, holding her legs so that she couldn't kick him but unable to prevent her thumping him on his back. Striding along with her, he yanked open the door and carried her down the corridor to her own room, but gasped and staggered as she dug him in the ribs. He dropped her onto her bed, but she was up in an instant and fighting him like a wildcat.

Her hands beat furiously against Milo for a while, but then the fight suddenly went out of her and she went limp. Milo went to the door, pretended to shut it and leave, but stayed where he was, watching her warily. Paige didn't look round, and her arms went round the pillow, holding it tightly, and she quietly began to cry.

His face suddenly wooden, Milo quietly went out of the room and left her alone.

CHAPTER NINE

MILO didn't sleep at all that night, didn't even attempt to. Going down to the drawing-room, he poured himself a stiff whisky, but after one swallow found that it tasted foul in his mouth. He threw it down the sink in the kitchen and took a long drink of water instead, his throat working. Restlessly he prowled round the house, looking at his pictures and trying to concentrate on them, but getting no pleasure from it. Remembering Paige's threats to go to the press and to make a scene at his office, he cursed and tried to think of a way of getting rid of her without any scandal or publicity. He could, in return, threaten to go to the press himself, he supposed. Show her up for the little cheat she was. But it was only a fleeting idea; they both knew that it was the last thing he wanted. She had made a fool of him in front of everyone once; he would be the laughing stock of the country if it happened again.

Still furious, trying to think of a way, Milo found that he had wandered down to the basement area again. The sauna was still on. Going over to the thermostat, he lowered the temperature, then hesitated before slowly opening the door.

It was like stepping back into the past. The wooden walls of the room seemed to have absorbed all the passion and desire, all the tension and the joyous fulfilment of that shining hour. His ears filled with their remembered cries, his heart with the hammering glory of his climax, of the knowledge that she was his at last. He had lived in yearning hope of that moment for so long, and when he had finally attained it he'd thought that his happiness was complete, and nothing could ever possibly plunge him back into despair.

And yet it had come so quickly, like some malignant fate laughing in his face, just waiting to strike him down again at the very cruellest moment of all. It was too much to bear. Milo gave a great groan, a bitter cry of despair, and beat his fists against the wall. Now his heart felt as if it had been brutally torn in two, as if it would never be whole again. And the pain, so deep and so agonising, coming as it did immediately on top of so much happiness, was like a living fire that consumed his spirit. He felt that he wasn't strong enough to bear it, that he couldn't go on living. But then anger and bitterness consumed him once again. He would conquer this, use the pain to fuel his hatred, make damn sure she paid for what she'd done to him.

It occurred to Milo then that if he kicked her out it would make that vengeance more difficult. Why not let her stay? At least then she would be under his eye and he would be able to take advantage of every opportunity that came along to retaliate. But then he thought of having to be physically near her, of having to smell her perfume, to look into those incredible eyes, to see her body and know what it was like to possess it. Perhaps she might try to seduce him again, would flaunt herself as she had before and make him unable to resist the temptation of taking her to bed. Sweat broke out on his lip and his pulses raced. Again the sounds of their lovemaking filled his ears. For several minutes he was lost, drowned in those thoughts, and he had to force himself to think only of revenge. But revenge, he found, could be sweet, and it gave

him vindictive pleasure in deciding what form that
revenge would take.

Milo left early for the office and didn't come home
until quite late. He half expected Paige to have left,
to have realised that there was no longer anything but
hate between them and it was useless to stay, but
when he let himself into the house he heard music
coming from the kitchen. Slowly he walked through
the house towards the sound.

   She was standing at the stove, concentrating on stirring the savoury-smelling contents of a saucepan, and
didn't hear him. She was wearing a short denim skirt
and a long sweater over which she'd tied one of his
blue-striped barbecue aprons. It was too big for her
and hung down below her skirt at the front, making
her look like a little girl dressing up in adult clothes.
A surge of sudden tenderness had to be fought down,
along with a fleeting glimpse of the daughter they
might have had. It left such a bitter taste in his mouth
that Milo needed nothing more to feed his malevo-
lence. He had made up his mind that he wanted her
to stay, but knew that she was clever, and would guess
the reason if he said so. So he must appear to want
the opposite.

   Striding into the kitchen, he said curtly, 'I told you
to get out.'

   Paige swung round with a start, a frightened look
on her face, as if she was afraid that he was going to
attack her. But when she saw him come to a standstill,
albeit with his hands on his hips, his body language
threatening, she visibly relaxed. Her chin came up.
'And I said I was staying.'

   'Hasn't it got through to you yet? I don't—'

'There's no point in going on,' she broke in. 'I won't listen.'

'Yes, you damn well will. I want you out of here.'

But Paige had put her hands over her ears and was glaring at him mutinously. It occurred to Milo that she was wearing more make-up than usual and at first he thought it was because she was trying to attract him—a thought that filled him with anger—but suddenly he realised it was to cover the puffiness around her eyes. Of course, he had left her crying last night. Old habits died hard; he found the memory and her brave attempt to hide it momentarily tugging at his heart. But all sentiment was swiftly buried beneath the greater hatred.

Folding his arms, he said scathingly, 'And just what do you hope to gain by staying here? By this—' he made a contemptuous gesture towards the cooker '—touching show of domesticity?'

'You know why I'm staying,' she said, her voice not quite steady. 'And I'm merely cooking dinner.'

'For yourself?'

Her eyes were watchful. 'For us both.'

'Really?' Milo gave a twisted smile. 'You can't satisfy my appetite for sex so you'll try my appetite for food, is that it?'

Flushes of colour came into her pale cheeks. 'You were more than satisfied,' she shot at him. 'So don't denigrate what we had.'

He laughed outright. 'How can anyone possibly denigrate something that was based on a lie from start to finish? It couldn't possibly get any more sordid than it is already.'

'I've told you the reasons why I acted the way I did. I don't intend to go into them again, and I'm certainly not going to grovel to you, if that's what you want,' she said with dignity.

'I'm not asking you to. All I want is for you to get out of my life.' And, turning on his heel, he strode out of the room and went upstairs to shower and change out of his business suit into more casual clothes.

When he came down the door to the dining-room was open. He saw that she had laid the table with a snow-white cloth, with his best silver, and a low bowl of flowers. Did she really think that he was going to fall for some feeble ploy like that? he thought contemptuously. She came out of the kitchen, said nervously, 'Dinner is ready.'

'OK.' He went and sat down at the table.

She hurried to bring in the first course. It was coquilles Saint-Jacques. Milo took one look at it and pushed the plate aside. 'I don't like cockles,' he said shortly.

Paige had hardly sat down. She raised her eyes to look into his, ready to be angry but not sure whether he was lying or not. But Milo just pushed his chair back and crossed his legs to sit there with an utterly bored expression. Tight-lipped, Paige began to eat, but kept glancing at him from under her lashes. She hadn't eaten very much before she got up and took the plates away, coming back shortly afterwards with a steaming tureen which she set in the centre of the table.

'I know you like this,' she said defiantly, 'because you've had it before. It's chicken Maryland.'

She took the lid off the tureen and went to pick up the serving spoon, but Milo quickly reached forward and got to it first. Standing up, he said sarcastically, 'No, let me. After all, you are a guest.' Dipping the spoon into the bowl, he slapped a great helping onto her plate, then another, the sauce splashing. 'In fact,' he said with malicious enjoyment, 'why don't you have it all?' Dropping the spoon, he picked up the bowl by its handles and upturned it over her plate.

The food cascaded out, overflowing the plate and oozing over the table, the damask cloth now stained beyond repair. Some of it trickled over onto the floor, but Paige wasn't looking at it. Her eyes were fixed on Milo's face and there was a pinched look to her mouth.

'That was an unbelievably cheap and stupid trick,' she said in cold anger.

'Well, you'd know all about that, wouldn't you?' Putting his hands on the table, he leaned towards her. 'Don't cook for me. Don't do anything for me. The only thing I want from you is for you to get out of this house!' Then he pushed himself upright and strode out, slamming the front door behind him.

He walked up to the Spaniards, had a meal and stayed there, finishing off a bottle of wine, until the place closed. He ought to have felt tight but he didn't. His mind was too full of anger to be anything other than razor-sharp. She hadn't locked him out as he thought she might have done, and he knew instinctively that she was still there. As she'd said when she'd inadvertently given herself away, he was psychic where she was concerned. He didn't bother to look in the dining-room to see if she'd cleaned up the mess, but went straight up to his room.

It came back to him now, that incident she'd been referring to last night. It must have been about fourteen years ago, when she was only six or seven, before her parents had split up and when her grandfather was still alive. The old man had brought her to the office but she'd got bored and had sneaked away to the boardroom where she'd sat in the chairman's seat and had started drawing all over the big blotter. Then she'd heard footsteps and had hastily hidden in a cupboard. But the footsteps had been his, and although he hadn't noticed anything amiss Milo had instinctively known that she was hidden away there. He had pulled her out, grinning, had said in the condescending way of an adult to a child, 'Come on, you imp of mischief, your grandfather's looking for you.'

Her eyes had been beautiful even then, he remembered as he stripped off his clothes and, naked, got into bed. The sheets were clean and felt crisp and cold. His whole body right through to his heart felt cold, and he didn't think that he would ever feel really warm again. Desperately trying not to think of last night, of the joy that he had known in this bed less than twenty-four hours ago, he concentrated on what had come after and eventually managed to fall asleep.

It was in the early hours of the morning that he woke in a primitive awareness of danger. He lay very still, his heart thudding, all his senses alert, knowing that there was someone in the room. But it was very dark; there was no moonlight shining through the curtains. Slowly, trying to keep his breathing even, he turned his head. It was Paige. He realised it at once, and with an angry movement lunged across the bed to turn on the lamps.

She didn't move, didn't even blink. He stared at her, then with stunned astonishment it came to him that she was sleepwalking. Her only garment was a cream silk nightgown that wasn't much more than a slip. It clung to the soft roundness of her breasts, followed the line of her waist and hips. His mouth went dry as he stared at her, wondering what to do, whether he should wake her or guide her back to her room. But, while he was searching his mind for anything he'd read on sleepwalking, she made a sound like a sob and put out an arm as if to get into bed. He was about to yell at her, but then she straightened, gave a long sigh, turned and walked away.

When she'd gone, Milo stared after her, hardly now able to credit what he'd seen. Had she really been sleepwalking? Or had it been a ploy, another of her cheap tricks? He lay back in bed, staring at the ceiling and wondering, either way, how he could turn it to his advantage.

The next morning he again went early to the office but spent a large part of the morning on the phone, putting in hand a couple of ideas that had nothing to do with work. He was due to make a trip to New York for a business conference but delegated it to someone else, who had to be briefed. Right now he wanted to be at home with Paige. That thought made his mouth twist in bitter irony. Two days ago he would have wanted to be home with her for the very best and most wonderful of reasons; now everything had changed completely. Towards the end of the afternoon the dealer Milo used in his art purchases rang to say that he'd eventually been successful in the commission Milo had given him that morning. 'It took a lot of persuasion,' he told Milo. 'But he eventually capitulated.'

'I suppose by a lot of persuasion you mean a lot of money,' Milo said dryly, and he whistled silently when he was told precisely how much.

'You did say to get it no matter what the price,' the man reminded him.

'Of course. Thanks. I'm pleased you managed to pull it off. I'll have a money order sent round to you at once and I'd like you to send someone to collect the picture tonight.'

'Tonight!' The dealer was amazed. 'But why?'

'A whim of mine,' Milo said evasively. Pyramiding his fingers, he gazed for a moment into space, a look of satisfaction in his eyes.

When he arrived home that evening he was carrying a corsage of an exquisite orchid in its florist's box. He left it on the hall table where Paige would be sure to notice it while he went up to change into his evening suit. When he ran down the staircase Paige was standing in the hall, a belligerent look on her face.

Seeing her, Milo began to hum a carefree tune, but broke off to say shortly, 'Still here?'

'If you're trying to make me jealous you won't succeed.'

He laughed. 'That wasn't my intention. I'm merely reorganising my life. Filling the gap you've left in it, if you like.'

'It was you who pushed me out,' she reminded him.

'Oh, I admit it was my fault,' he said casually, making her frown in puzzlement. 'I should never have gone on looking for you when you walked out. It would have been far better to let you stay as an unsolved mystery. Yes, I blame myself,' he murmured. 'I should have listened to that old adage Once bitten, twice shy.' He glanced at her. 'I'm sure you agree?'

He watched her as she seemed to consider her answer. There was something about her face that was familiar—not her features, which he would always know by heart, but something else he couldn't put his finger on.

'We could talk about it,' she said carefully.

Milo smiled coldly and turned to the mirror over the hall table to check his tie. 'There is nothing I could possibly want to discuss with you, except to know when you're leaving,' he said acidly. As he gazed at his reflection while straightening his tie it suddenly came to him. What he had recognised in Paige's face was something that he had seen in his own reflection for many long months after she'd run away: bleak helplessness coupled with an inner torment, an inner rage against fate, which had somehow to be held down and controlled. He gave an involuntary gasp, then blinked and looked away. Serve her damn well right, he thought viciously.

The buzzer from the intercom on the gate sounded and he crossed to it, spoke to the taxi driver and told him to come up to the house. When he heard the cab draw up outside he opened the door and went out to greet his date.

'Milo!' The woman who got out of the taxi was dark-haired, slender, and beautifully dressed as always. 'How lovely to see you again—and so unexpected!' She gave him an arch look from under her lashes.

'Come inside.' Taking her hand, Milo kissed her lightly, then led her into the house and shut the door. 'Let's have a drink.'

He went towards the drawing-room, but the woman stopped when she saw Paige and looked at Milo enquiringly.

Coming to a halt, he said offhandedly, 'Oh, this is Paige Chandos. You may have read about her in the tabloids. And this is Alison Reynolds,' he said to Paige. 'I think you've seen her once before—in a restaurant,' he added meaningfully. He saw Paige flush and felt some satisfaction at the sight, but then he ignored her as he put a familiar arm round Alison's waist and took her into the drawing-room.

Paige was gone when they left to go to the ballet, and he hoped that he had managed to upset her. But while they watched the performance whatever small triumph he had felt completely evaporated. He had booked the tickets because Paige had said how much she wanted to see it, and it should have been she who was by his side, not this old flame who had passed on to other men. When he glanced at Alison she turned her head to smile at him, and pressed her leg against his. He was momentarily sickened by the action and by the knowledge in her eyes, and couldn't help comparing her to Paige, who was so innocent, so unused—and so damn stubborn. He felt confused, but was angry at himself for being so. It was all clear-cut; she had deliberately set out to hurt and punish him for wrongs that existed only in her imagination. She hadn't given him a chance, and he was damned if he would give her one now.

They had dinner at a nightclub after the ballet, Alison enjoying talking about old times, the fun they'd had. But to Milo she might just as well have been talking about two entirely different people, so alien and so unmemorable did it all appear in retrospect. It seemed now that his life had only really started when Paige and her grandmother had come back from India. He had fallen for her so completely, but had been intimidated by her youth and the almost cloistered way she'd been brought up into cocooning her and respecting her innocence. He hadn't realised that she was already a woman in her instincts and needs, had instead put her on the pedestal that her grandmother had demanded.

Not that he'd made that mistake when he'd found her again, he thought bleakly. But by then it was too late, of course. It occurred to him that he had known

Paige almost as three different people—first as a
child, then as the girl he had fallen in love with,
whose outlook on life had been so simple, so full of
expectation, and thirdly as the woman he had found
in France, a woman of irresistible beauty, but who had
stooped to a devious trick, to living a lie. She's like
a book, he thought, and wondered how many more
Paiges there were to be turned, then twisted his lip at
the grossness of his own pun.

'Hey! A penny for them.' Alison was recalling his
attention.

'Sorry. I was thinking about the ballet,' he lied.
'What did you think of the solo in the second half?'

She answered him but he wasn't really listening.
As he lifted his glass to his mouth, it came to him
that the trick he himself was playing tonight wasn't
exactly edifying for any of the three people concerned, but his anger was such that there was no way
he wanted to draw back.

They danced in the dimly lit room, holding each
other close, and it was gone two before they found a
cab and he gave Alison's address. In the taxi she put
her hand in his and nestled close to him. He didn't
kiss her, but then he wouldn't have kissed a woman
in a taxi anyway, his mind rebelling at being so de-
monstrative under some stranger's amused glance.
Alison was living at the same flat as when he'd known
her before. Keeping hold of his hand, she said, 'You
are coming up for coffee,' making it a statement
rather than a question.

The flat was much the same as he remembered
it—the sitting-room with its modern furniture where
Alison let him help her off with her jacket and then
turned within his arms to kiss him, the bedroom with
its king-size bed where she soon led him...

*   *   *

'Damn it all to hell!' Milo said in violent fury. It was half an hour later and he was standing on the pavement outside Alison's building. His hands were thrust into his pockets along with his tie, his shirt was open at the neck and he gave every sign of having dressed in a hurry.

It was raining quite heavily and there was no sign of a cab even if he had been in the mood to go home, which he definitely wasn't. Turning up the collar of his jacket against the rain, he strode along the street, his hands still in his pockets and his soul consumed with rage. He had tried to put Paige completely out of his head—God, how he'd tried!—but she was always there, like some ghost haunting his mind, coming between him and Alison's willing and expectant body. He swore again and blamed Paige entirely. He couldn't make love to another woman.

It had been his intention to stay out all night and there was no way he was going back to the house. So he turned his steps towards the City, walking through streets that were empty except for the dossers sleeping in shop doorways and the occasional all-night double-decker trundling along. When he reached his office building the security guard let him in, trying to hide his surprise at seeing the managing director in soaking wet evening clothes and with the grimmest look on his face the man had ever seen.

'A parcel arrived for you, sir,' the guard told him. 'Brought by special messenger.'

'Thanks. Give me a hand with it, will you?'

Between them they carried the large thin rectangular parcel up to his office, then Milo took a shower in the executive cloakroom and changed into a spare suit and shirt that he always kept there. He unpacked the parcel carefully, already knowing it was the pic-

ture he'd bought. It was the portrait of Paige, done by
Jean-Louis, the picture she'd been sure he would
never sell. But he had sold it, although it had cost a
great deal. Whether he would have done so if he'd
known Milo was the buyer was an unanswered question, but Milo had gone through the dealer so his
name hadn't been mentioned.

Propping the picture on a table against the wall,
Milo stood silently looking at it for a long time. He
was trying to work out which Paige had sat for this
portrait, the innocent girl or the vindictive woman, but
it seemed to be neither. This was a woman who
seemed to be apart from the modern background, the
centre of it but not of it. She seemed to be ignoring
everything around her and looking almost eagerly out,
her eyes full of something that he saw with surprise
was very close to hope. But what was she hoping for?
That Jean-Louis would fall in love with her, marry
her? Or could she, deep in her subconscious, be hoping that he, Milo, would see it?

That idea came as a shock and was instantly dis-
missed, but her eyes seemed to follow him all the
hours the painting stood in his office that day, compelling his own to return to it constantly. His use for
the painting had been clear-cut, he had known exactly
what he intended to do with it, but now he hesitated,
and then made a phone call and had the picture taken
out of his sight.

When he got home that evening Paige made no
mention of his having been out all the previous night.
She had cooked a meal, but Milo had deliberately
stopped for a Chinese take-away on the way home,
and ate the meal off a tray in the sitting-room while
watching television. He was desperately tired after his
sleepless night, and the rich food and the wine he'd

drunk with it made him even more sleepy, so that he dozed in his chair. He woke to find Paige reaching out to take the tray from him. Immediately he caught her wrist, gripping it until she let go of the tray with a cry. Only then did he loosen his grip.

She stood back, biting her lip. Milo didn't say anything, just stared at her, and after a moment she swung away and ran out of the room.

Milo went to his study immediately afterwards, feeling that he'd won a small battle. He did some work that couldn't wait before going up to his room. He saw that Paige's light was still on as he passed her door, but he went to bed and fell asleep almost immediately. It was about three in the morning when he woke, again with the feeling that someone was in the room. This time he had left the curtains open and there was moonlight shining through the window so that he was able to see Paige standing just inside the door again. Moving carefully so as not to wake her, he turned over and watched.

She came to the side of the bed as she had done before, and stood there as if waiting for something. Softly, he said, 'Paige?'

Turning eagerly at the sound, she reached out a groping hand. Milo took it and drew her closer.

'Do you want to come to bed, Paige?'

She didn't speak, just pulled back the covers and got into bed beside him.

Was she really asleep or was this just another act? He was almost certain that she was, and the idea of having her in bed with him, compliant but unconscious, sent a thrill of lustful excitement running through him. He could do what he liked to her and she would never know—unless she woke and found it happening, of course. The thought of the shock that would give her amused him, until he realised that she might be pleased by it, that she'd see it as weakness on his part. Maybe that was why she was here; maybe it was what she wanted, even subconsciously. Milo stared moodily at her head against the whiteness of the pillow. After the way she'd deceived him so successfully, there was no way he could take anything on trust.

To test her, he put a hand on her breast. Paige gave a small sigh and turned her head towards him, and he saw that her eyes were open but staring, as if her gaze had become fixed, almost like a blind person who saw only darkness. He began to caress her and she murmured something, then gave a low moan, her lips pouting as if expecting to be kissed. Tempted to do so, Milo leaned over her. She looked very beautiful in the silvered light, her hair spread over the pillow. Desire seethed through him, burning into his stomach. He wanted to take her and to hell with the consequences. He let his hand wander over her and she gave a purr of contentment, her body arching towards his exploring fingers. The need to take her was almost uncontrollable, filling his loins, threatening to overwhelm his senses.

But he couldn't do it. Even though he had every reason to despise her, and she certainly deserved everything she got, he just couldn't take advantage of her when she wasn't aware of what was happening. Deeply frustrated, he threw himself back against the pillow, then, determined to get some advantage out of this, he reached out to the bedside table and picked up the pen that he always kept by the phone.

Throwing back the covers, he said softly in her ear, 'Paige. Turn over for me.'

Obediently, she did so.

His hand unsteady, Milo pulled up her silk night-dress to reveal her behind. It was such a gorgeous little behind, so beautifully pale and rounded, that he almost gave way to temptation. He had to stifle a groan, but then wrote his name in large letters on the soft, velvet-smooth curves.

Getting out of bed, he took her hand and said firmly, 'Come on, Paige, back to bed.'

She made protesting noises but let him lead her back to her room, and got into bed when he told her to, like a small, good child. Milo looked down at her for a long moment, then abruptly turned and went back to his own room, where he stuck a chair under the door handle so that she couldn't get in again, and immediately went and stood under the shower, letting the cold water freeze out desire.

For what was left of the night Milo dozed only fitfully, and got up early to go down to the gym to work out, following up the routine with a long swim in the pool.

It seemed that Paige, too, had got up early. When he'd dressed she was in the kitchen, making break-fast—just for herself, he noted. And she hadn't bothered to cook anything, was just pouring cereal into a bowl. Looking at her face, he saw that there were dark shadows around her eyes.

'My, my,' he commented. 'You do look tired. Must be your guilty conscience.' She shot him a look but didn't rise to the barb, so he went on with inner enjoyment, 'Or could it be that you didn't sleep very well?'

'I slept perfectly well,' Paige said shortly, sitting down at the table.

Pouring himself some orange juice, Milo sat down opposite her, which was strange, because nowadays he usually avoided her like the plague. He smiled, making her gaze at him suspiciously, then slowly shook his head. 'No, you didn't.'

'Didn't what?'

'Didn't sleep very well.'

She stared at him, her eyes wary, beginning to be nervous. 'What do you mean?'

His smile malicious now, Milo said, 'I mean that you didn't spend the whole night in your own bed.'

She gasped, said angrily, 'What are you trying to say?'

'Why, merely that you went for a walk in the night—straight to my door. And not only came into my room, but also into my bed.'

For a moment she was too consumed by anger to speak, then threw down her spoon and got to her feet. 'You cheapskate liar! What kind of trick is this?'

'No trick,' Milo returned calmly. 'You were sleepwalking. You came to my bed and we—er—took it from there.'

Her cheeks fiery with rage, Paige said, 'I don't believe you. I'd have known if— You're just making this up. Of all the underhand, nasty, lying—'

'I can prove it,' Milo said, his voice soft but the words cutting her off in mid-flow.

Reaching out, she gripped the edge of the table. 'What do you mean?'

'Have you looked at yourself in the mirror this morning?'

'Of course.'

'No, I mean, your whole length, without clothes on, of course.'

Her eyes were fixed on his face, full of dread. 'What have you done?'

'Why don't you go and take a look?'

She continued to stare at him for a couple of minutes, still not certain whether to believe him, but something in his face—his enjoyment probably—must have convinced her, because Paige suddenly turned on her heel and ran upstairs.

'Don't forget to turn round,' he called after her.

The sound of her footsteps faded and Milo could imagine her rushing into her room and stripping off her clothes, searching for bruise or finger marks, finding none, and then turning round. He wondered what her reaction would be, whether it would drive her away. He hoped not, because he hadn't finished with her yet.

Five minutes later Paige came tearing down the stairs, so fast that he hardly had time to stand up before she exploded into the kitchen, yelling and screaming at him, and at the same time trying to rain blows at his head. He managed to grab one of her wrists, turned her round so that she had her back to him, and pinioned her arms against her sides while he lifted her off the ground. She continued to kick and yell, struggling wildly, so that it took all his strength to hold her.

It was a while before her strength gave out and only then did she give up. She became still in his hold and he slowly lowered her until her feet were on the floor. 'What did you do to me?' she demanded in a low, strained voice.

Milo toyed with telling her a lie, making out that they'd had sex. Why shouldn't she suffer by being lied to? He'd certainly suffered enough from the lies she'd told him. But then he said harshly, 'I did nothing. I didn't want you.' He felt her stiffen, saw her face go white. Knowing his rejection had got to her, he added cruelly, 'Although I could have done. It wasn't the first time you've come to my room in the night.'

'Let go of me.' Milo did so and Paige turned to face him, a stricken look in her eyes. 'Is that true?'

'Why should I bother to make it up? You're the liar around here. Remember?'

If a look could have annihilated, Milo would have been a small heap of ash. Without a word, Paige turned and walked away, but this time her head came up and there was immense dignity in the set of her shoulders. Milo watched her go, trying to ignore the unwanted stirring in his heart.

She was up in her room for a long time and Milo fully expected her to come down with her bags packed, but when she finally came downstairs Paige was dressed for a day in town. She didn't speak to him but went straight out to a waiting taxi. It was Saturday and ordinarily Milo would have gone on a prowl round the art galleries or, as it was still the season, to watch a rugby match. Today, though, he didn't feel like it. He set himself to finish the work he'd brought home from the office, but couldn't settle to it, so sat around and read the papers, then fixed himself some lunch and wondered where Paige had gone, whether she was looking for somewhere else to stay or if she would go back to France and Jean-Louis.

It was late afternoon before Paige came back. She had her own key, and let herself in. Milo was in the sitting-room and would have had to get up from his chair to see her. He wanted to but forced himself to stay in his seat. Paige didn't come in but went straight upstairs, and he didn't see her again until the early evening when he himself had been up to change for a night at the opera. He had two tickets but he was going alone, although he wouldn't let Paige know that, of course. She was already down in the hall, phoning for a taxi, when he came down.

Milo was running lightly down the stairs when he saw her and his steps slowed. She looked absolutely stunning. The dress she was wearing must have been the result of her shopping trip that day; it was a long sleeveless dress, basically a black sheath but with a wide white collar that plunged to cross over just above her waist, revealing a suggestive and tantalising amount of cleavage. And she'd had her hair cut into a much more elegant style. In some ways she looked more like the girl he remembered from when they'd been engaged, but now she was a very chic and sophisticated young woman. Entirely a woman, he thought wryly, knowing that he'd taken her virginity.

She was holding the phone in her left hand and he suddenly realised that she was no longer wearing Jean-Louis's ring. That raised all kinds of speculations in his mind; had she broken off her engagement? Had Jean-Louis?

But only Paige could tell him, so, hoping to find out and also to learn where she was going, when she'd put the phone down, Milo said, 'Going to the West End? Shall we share a cab?'

'Call your own,' Paige said shortly, and walked away from him.

It irked him not to know where she was going—or who with. The opera, *Tosca*, was one of his favourites but Milo found it difficult to concentrate, let alone lose himself in the music and singing. There was too much on his mind, too many unanswered questions going through his head. Afterwards he went to a gaming club where he found several people he knew and passed away another couple of hours until he felt he could go home without losing face. But Paige wasn't home and didn't come in until about three in the morning, when he was already in bed.

From then on she kept out of his way and hardly looked at him, let alone spoke. But she didn't leave. Milo noticed, though, that she looked very tired, and he wondered if it was because she was trying to prevent herself from sleepwalking again. Often he lay awake, listening, but he kept the chair propped against the door and was pretty sure she hadn't tried to get in again. He knew that a cash buyer had been found for the house in Chelsea and that the sale would soon go through. Was that what she was waiting for? Would she collect the money and then go back to Jean-Louis? But she wasn't wearing his ring; that must mean something, surely? Unless she'd simply lost it, of course. Angrily Milo tried to push her out of his mind and concentrate on his work, but found that he was thinking about her as much as he had when she'd first disappeared. But somehow it was worse now, because he'd been intimate with her, knew her body, and couldn't forget the pleasure they'd shared.

It was about ten days later, when spring had suddenly but definitely arrived, that he brought the picture home with him from work one evening. Paige had gone out—where, he didn't know—and it was gone midnight when she came in. He had hung the picture in the hall, in place of the mirror, so that she would be sure to see it. He heard a taxi pull up, her key in the lock, and strolled out into the hall so that he could see her reaction.

Paige was standing in front of the picture, staring up at it, a black cape that she'd been taking off hanging in her hand. Slowly, her face white and pinched, she turned to look at Milo as he lounged in the door-way. She didn't speak, but her eyes were one giant question.

Putting his hands in his pockets, he walked to her side. 'He sold it to me,' he said casually. 'Evidently the money meant more than the *sentimental* value.' He stressed the word, making it like a sneer, delib-erately denigrating any feelings that had existed be-tween Jean-Louis and herself. 'Admittedly he didn't know I was the buyer, but he didn't hesitate when it came to selling it.'

Paige flinched a little but her chin came up and she said sarcastically, 'Rather an expensive way of scor-ing a cheap point, isn't it?'

'You think I bought it just to prove to you how little Jean-Louis cares? Oh, no, I had quite a different reason.'

Her fatigue-smudged eyes immediately filled with suspicion. When he didn't speak she became angry and said, 'All right, so why? I know you just can't wait to tell me about the latest cruelty your twisted little mind has cooked up.'

His jaw hardening at that, Milo said shortly, 'The picture is a complete fiction. You're depicted as in-nocent, naive, but all the time you were living a life of pure deception. You were certainly deceiving Jean-Louis; what he saw in you didn't even exist.'

She was wearing a touch of blusher but her face had gone so pale that it looked completely unnatural. 'What are you saying?' The question was almost a whisper, it was so low and full of dread.

'That if what the picture depicts doesn't exist, then nor should the picture.'

'No!' A surge of pure anger flamed in her eyes. 'I won't let you destroy it.'

Moving between him and the picture, Paige spread out her arms to protect it. But Milo laughed and, catching her arm with his left hand, he jerked her out of the way. At the same time he took a small bottle from his pocket and, working out the cork with his thumb, he threw the contents at the picture, aiming at the face.

'No!'

Paige screamed out the word and broke from his hold. She tried to reach out to the picture and for one terrible moment Milo thought she was going to try to wipe off the acid with her bare hands. Quickly he caught her and held her with her back to him, forcing her to watch as the acid etched into the paint, bubbling and hissing, the colours combining as they melted and began to run into one another, trickling down the un-touched part of the canvas and leaving long, sticky trails of what had once been a work of art and was now reduced to a mess of oil paint. What had once been a beautiful face was nothing now but a distorted caricature of misshapen ugliness.

'You bastard!' Paige wrenched herself free. 'That was his best work! The greatest thing he'd ever done. And you destroyed it out of petty, small-minded spite! How could you?' She put her hands over her face for a moment, overcome by sobs of mingled bitterness and rage. 'God, and to think that I loved you! *So much.* I must have been mad, completely blind. You're just a self-centred hypocrite. You're supposed to love art and yet you could destroy a picture of that quality just to get back at me!'

She was so genuinely upset, so bitter, that his heart smote him and he reached out to her. 'Paige, wait. I—'

But she knocked his hand aside contemptuously.

'Well, you've got what you wanted. I'm not going to hang around any longer to be punished by you. Because I don't care any more. I'm through. Go to hell your own way!' Grabbing up her bag and wrap, she headed for the door, fumbling with the catch.

'Paige! Wait a minute.' Milo tried to grab her but only succeeded in getting hold of her wrap. She got the door open and for a moment they had a tug of war, but with an angry exclamation Paige let go and he fell back, the cape in his hands and her bag falling to the floor.

Quickly he followed, but she was already flying down the drive. Milo had to stop and lock the door before he could chase after her. But when he got to the gate she was running hard down the street. He raced along, faster than she could go, and knew that he would soon catch her. But when Paige heard him she glanced round, then deliberately turned off the road and headed into the lonely darkness of the open heath.

CHAPTER TEN

PAIGE didn't keep to the path but ran across the grass towards the bushes. She paused for a brief moment and Milo thought she'd come to her senses and was going to stop, but it was only to kick off her shoes. He was about to yell at her but then thought better of it; he didn't want to attract any unwelcome attention from the drop-outs that lived on the heath or the perverts who frequented it after dark, as they did any open space in London.

As she reached the bushes, her figure was lost in the darkness, and he was filled with the fear that he wouldn't be able to find her, that she would hide and he would lose her. But he was fit and strong and burst into the bushes before she'd had time to look for a hiding place. He heard her give a sob before she ran on. Was she still crying, then? Had what he'd done hurt her so much? He raced on, desperate to keep her within sight, but caught his foot in a tree root and stumbled, almost falling. Cursing, Milo picked himself up and went on.

Leaving the shelter of the bushes, Paige was running across a part of the heath that bordered a lake. There were trees round its edge but they were tall and offered no hiding place, only creating deeper patches of shadow where it was impossible to see her flying figure until she emerged on the other side. Her anger seemed to have given her wings; it was taking Milo all his time to catch her up after his stumble, his feet making no sound over the grass.

He too went into the shadow of the trees, and when he looked past them his blood ran cold. Two other figures, quite obviously masculine, had appeared near the lake. They must have seen Paige and started to run forward, cutting her off. She stopped precipitately, and with fervent relief Milo saw her turn as if to run back towards him. But then she hesitated, changed her mind and ran at right angles, away from both him and the two men. Immediately they changed course to cut her off, but their eyes were all on Paige, and they hadn't yet seen Milo coming through the trees.

She was running hard but was tiring now, her breath coming in ragged, gasping pants that he could hear through the stillness of the night. Suddenly one of the men moved to her right and she veered away, but it had enabled the other to come close and with a leap he grabbed her. Swung round, she hit out at him, but his laugh of triumph reached Milo and he knew they'd got her. In an agony of fear for her, he flew across the piece of open ground and launched himself full tilt at the man who held her. He let go in startled amazement and turned to face his attacker.

'Run, Paige!' Milo yelled at her as he grappled with the man.

The other man, thin and slight, came rushing up to help his friend. Neither of them was big and Milo thought that he wouldn't have too much trouble, but he didn't like the confident way they came at him. 'Clear off! She's ours,' one of them yelled at him.

'That's where you're wrong, you little rat. She's mine,' Milo grated as his fist connected with the man's jaw.

The man grunted and doubled up, backed off. Swinging round to face the other attacker, Milo saw with renewed fear that Paige was still there. 'Run,' he shouted at her again. 'Run, my love.'

But then all his attention was taken up with fighting off both men as they came at him again. He was dealing out punches, trying to watch them both, but one came round behind him. Suddenly the man backed off, snarling, as Paige leapt on his back and put her arm across his eyes, her other round his neck, choking him. Milo managed to floor the man he was fighting and turned to help Paige, but the man had already thrown her off and she lay on the ground. With a sick surge of fear Milo ran to her, but the man turned on him with an obscene oath and took him momentarily off guard. Milo felt a blow and immediately hit back. The man staggered away, ignoring his friend who still lay on the ground, and took himself off into the darkness of the bushes.

Milo stood panting over the unconscious attacker and Paige got up and ran to him. 'Milo!' Throwing her arms round him, she held him close. 'Oh, God! Oh, God.'

'Are you all right?'

'Yes. But if you hadn't been here...! I was so scared.'

He was fumbling in his pocket, found it difficult. 'In my pocket,' he rasped. 'You'll find a mobile phone. Call the police.' She found it, her hands trembling, but managed to dial 999. 'Better tell them to send an ambulance as well,' Milo said unsteadily.

Paige gave him a startled glance then looked down at the fallen man. 'Why? Is he dead?'

Milo laughed, and thought how strange his voice sounded. 'To hell with him. The little bastard has stabbed me.' And he sank to his knees.

*   *   *

He managed to stay conscious until the police came, afraid that the second assailant might come back and attack Paige again. She used her slip as a wad to staunch the blood that flowed from his chest, trying to be brave but unable to stop the sobs of terror that gathered in her throat. When he was in the ambulance he was able to give way to the pain at last, and fell in and out of consciousness as the vehicle raced through the night. Paige was there, he knew; he could feel her willing him to hold on, almost hear the words that screamed in her mind.

He moved his hand and she put hers into it, and in a moment of pure contentment he slipped into complete oblivion.

When he came to he found himself hooked up to tubes and wires leading to drips and machines. They made him feel ridiculous, like something out of a cheap Frankenstein film. He was going to complain about it but felt a deathly lethargy. He'd never felt so tired in his entire life. A nurse came, spoke to him, and he tried to answer her but found he hadn't the strength for even that. He wanted to see Paige, but it seemed she wasn't there. The nurse soothed him, told him to rest, and he thought he would like that very much. He felt so damn tired.

Paige waited at the hospital nearly all night. They operated on Milo straight away and afterwards they let her see him for a short while. But he was still unconscious and looked so terribly pale. He was in Intensive Care, and the very words frightened her to death. And no one would give her a definite answer when she asked them how he was, which frightened her even more.

The duty nurse persuaded her to go and have a lie

down in a room that they kept for relatives but she couldn't sleep, kept wandering back to the unit until the nurse insisted she go away. 'Go home and come back tomorrow,' the nurse told her. 'Look at you— your dress is torn and you're all dirty. Do you want him to see you like that?'

So Paige collected his keys and went back to the house. It seemed so big and empty without him there. Even when they had hated each other the most he had always been there, solid and secure. But how easily that security had been punctured, just with one stab of a knife. She glanced at the picture, the catalyst that had brought them back together but which Milo had also used as the means of finally driving her away. It was completely irreparable, anyone could see that, and she felt sad about it. But not about Jean-Louis. She had broken off her engagement to him the day after she and Milo had first made love. He had pro- tested, of course, declared that he was completely heartbroken, but she didn't believe him. His pride was hurt a little, perhaps, but not his heart. She wouldn't be at all surprised if he now wooed his rich American widow. Turning away, she felt indescribably lonely as she went to go upstairs. But then Paige hesitated. Her bag was still lying on the floor where she'd dropped it the previous night; from it she took a piece of paper, then went over to the phone. It was a while before it was answered, and her voice was very husky as she said, 'Mother? It's Paige.'

Their conversation wasn't very long, considering all the years, all the estrangement between them. They were both too emotional to be able to hold any kind of conversation, but the first step had been taken and Paige knew she was no longer on her own. Quickly then she ran to shower and change into a smart coral

dress that she thought would cheer Milo up. If he was
well enough to care. She shivered, but was sustained
by two words. When he'd come to her rescue and told
her to run, he'd added 'my love'. And by doing so
he'd made sure that she would never run from him
again. Eager to see him, Paige called a cab to take
her back to the hospital.

She'd hoped that she would be able to see Milo as
soon as she arrived but was told by the day duty nurse
that she would have to wait. 'The doctors are with
him now.'

So at least she would find out how he was. Paige
waited impatiently and stood up in eager anxiety
when she saw the white-coated men come out of the
unit. But they were talking together in low tones and
walked right by her. Overcome with fear, she looked
desperately round for someone to ask, someone to tell
her he was all right, he was going to live. That he
would get well and again be the man she'd always
loved. At last a nurse came along the corridor with a
man in a dark suit and Paige ran up to them. 'Please.
Mr Caine? How is he? The doctors didn't say. I've
been waiting so long.'

The two looked at her rather strangely, then the
man excused himself and went into the unit where
Milo lay.

'Who was that?' Paige demanded wildly. 'Why can
he go in and not me?'

'He's the hospital chaplain,' the nurse told her,
leading her away.

Paige felt as if the bones in her legs had melted.
'Is he—is he dead?'

'No, he isn't dead.' The nurse helped her to sit
down, found her a cup of tea, then said she'd go and
see if she could find out anything.

But it was the chaplain who came to seek her out. Looking at her keenly, he said, 'It seems that you and Mr Caine were once going to be married.'

'Yes, that's right.' She frowned, but then said, 'Do you know how he is? No one will tell me anything.'

'I spoke to him. He wants to marry you.'

Paige gave a gasping laugh, hope filling her heart. 'He does?'

'Yes. Today. Now.'

She stared, her face stricken, taking in the full import of what he was saying. 'Now?' she whispered.

'Yes. It seems that you already have a licence so there's no reason why it can't go ahead straight away. That's if you're willing, of course.'

'Willing? Yes. Yes, *of course* I am. But Milo? Is there—is there nothing that can be done?'

'It would appear not,' the man said kindly. 'It seems his case is hopeless.'

She nodded, trying to take it in, trying not to think how quickly her world had changed.

'It will take a little while to arrange,' he told her.

So Paige sat quietly alone in a room, aware that there was a flurry of activity outside. She knew now that there was nothing in the world she wanted more than to marry Milo, and it seemed that that, too, was his fervent wish. She prayed that he would have the strength to go through with it and that she would have the courage to be brave for his sake. A black wall of despair hit her when she thought of the time they'd wasted when she'd run away, for reasons that now seemed so stupid and futile. But those thoughts she pushed resolutely out of her mind; there would be a long, cold future in which there would be an eternity to dwell on what might have been.

At last a nurse came for her and gave her a posy of white roses to hold.

They had transformed the room into a bower of flowers. Dimly Paige was aware of them but had eyes only for Milo. He had been propped up on his pillows and looked deathly pale. The bed was raised high and the tubes and things had gone, were useless now. The chaplain had changed into his robes and there were several nurses there to act as witnesses, all of them misty-eyed. She wanted to rush to Milo, hold him, tell him how much she loved him, but instead walked slowly forward and took her place by his side. Turning his head a little, he managed to smile at her, his eyes full of love and tenderness. She smiled back at him; words were unimportant after all.

The ceremony was very simple but very moving. Milo even had a ring ready to slip onto her finger and said his vows in a voice that was firm, but for him very weak. Paige knew that her own voice trembled but he was being so brave that it gave her courage, although she had to blink back tears when the chaplain pronounced them man and wife and she leaned down to kiss his pale cheek.

Afterwards everyone left them alone, the chaplain carefully closing the door and shutting out the rest of the world.

Milo gave a long sigh, took hold of her wrist and said, 'Got you! At last.' His grip was surprisingly strong and his voice suddenly much more normal. Paige turned to look at him and found him grinning widely. She stared, her thoughts chaotic, but had no time to work anything out before he pulled her towards him, saying, 'Come here, woman, and let me kiss you properly.'

Putting his arms round her, he began to kiss her,

but she struggled free. 'Milo? *Milo*!' Straightening up, she stared at him and suddenly saw it all. 'You louse! You rotten… I thought you were dying!'

He laughed. 'Told you I'd get my own back one day. And how else is a man supposed to get married when you keep running out on me?' he complained.

'I do not keep… I will never forgive you for this! Do you know what I've been going through out there?' She stopped abruptly, realising that he must have gone through a whole year of nights like that. He was watching her quizzically, and relaxed when she slowly smiled. 'Just how badly are you hurt?'

Picking up her left hand, he touched the ring he'd so recently put on her third finger. 'It just so happens I always carried this around with me in my inside pocket. Sort of talisman. It deflected the knife so that it missed anything vital. I just bled a lot, that's all.'

Leaning her elbows on the bed, she propped her chin on them as she looked at him. 'So just how long will we have to wait until we can go on honeymoon?'

His eyes lit up. 'You in a hurry?' he asked.

She shrugged one shoulder. 'Could be.'

'Well, if you'll come a little closer…'

She did so and he put his hand behind her head to kiss her, then lowered it to her waist and drew her onto the bed.

'Milo! What are you doing? We can't!' She was shocked but laughing.

'Of course we can. It's what marriage beds are for.'

'But your wound?'

'You might have to help, do some work,' he acknowledged, undoing the zip of her dress.

'But somebody might come in.'

'They won't. I've made sure of that,' he said with certainty.

'You are a conniving, underhand rat—and I absolutely adore you.'

'Thank God for that.' And he kissed her deeply.

But a few minutes later Paige pushed herself away from him. 'Oh, no, you don't! I've just remembered—you destroyed my portrait.'

'Idiot!' He pulled her down again. 'It was only a copy. Do you really think I'd destroy a painting of the woman I've waited for all my life, the only woman I've ever loved?'

'Really?' she asked mistily.

'Really. Now, how about you getting down to some work?'

'You think we ought to consummate the marriage?'

He kissed her throat, said thickly, 'Definitely.' Adding with a wicked grin, 'Then the company will be all mine.'

Paige gave an outraged laugh that was half a sob of utter happiness. 'You know something? I'm glad you're going to live,' she told him. And got down to work.

MILLS & BOON®

Next Month's Romances

♡

Each month you can choose from a wide variety of romance novels from Mills & Boon®. Below are the new titles to look out for next month from the Presents™ and Enchanted™ series.

Presents™

Enchanted™

On sale from 4th May 1998

H1 9804

Available at most branches of
WH Smith, John Menzies, Martins, Tesco,
Asda, Volume One, Sainsbury and Safeway

NORA ROBERTS

Hot Ice

She had the cash and the connections. He knew
the whereabouts of a fabulous hidden fortune. It
was a business proposition, pure and simple.
Now all they needed to do was stay one step
ahead of their murderous rivals.

*"...her stories have fuelled the dreams of
25 million readers"*—Entertainment Weekly

1-55166-395-3
AVAILABLE FROM APRIL 1998

MARY LYNN BAXTER

Raw Heat

Successful broadcast journalist Juliana Reed is caught
in a web of corruption, blackmail and murder. Texas
Ranger, Gates O'Brien—her ex-husband—is the only
person she can turn to. Both know that getting out
alive is just the beginning...

*"Baxter's writing...strikes every chord within
the female spirit."*
—Bestselling author Sandra Brown

1-55166-394-5
AVAILABLE FROM APRIL 1998

MIRA®

DANCE FEVER

How would you like to win a year's supply of Mills & Boon®
books? Well you can and they're FREE! Simply complete the
competition below and send it to us by 31st October 1998.
The first five correct entries picked after the closing date will
each win a year's subscription to the Mills & Boon series of
their choice. What could be easier?

OBLARMOL
AMBUR
RTOXTFO
RASQUE
GANCO

KOPLA
OOOOMTLCIN
MALOENCF
SITWT
LASSA

EVJI
TAZLW
ACHACH
SCDIO
MAABS

G	R	I	H	C	H	A	R	J	T	O	N
O	P	A	R	L	H	U	B	P	I	B	W
M	O	O	R	L	L	A	B	M	C	V	H
B	L	D	I	O	O	K	C	L	U	P	E
R	K	U	B	N	C	R	Q	H	V	R	Z
S	A	N	I	O	O	N	G	W	A	S	V
T	S	I	N	R	M	G	E	U	B	G	H
W	L	G	H	S	O	R	Q	M	M	B	L
I	A	P	N	O	T	S	L	R	A	H	C
S	S	L	U	K	I	A	S	F	S	L	S
T	O	R	T	X	O	F	O	X	T	R	F
G	U	I	P	Z	N	D	I	S	C	O	Q

D8C

Please turn over for details of how to enter ⇨

HOW TO ENTER

There is a list of fifteen mixed up words overleaf, all of which when unscrambled spell popular dances. When you have unscrambled each word, you will find them hidden in the grid. They may appear forwards, backwards or diagonally. As you find each one, draw a line through it. Find all fifteen and fill in the coupon below then pop this page into an envelope and post it today. Don't forget you could win a year's supply of Mills & Boon® books—you don't even need to pay for a stamp!

Mills & Boon Dance Fever Competition
FREEPOST CN81, Croydon, Surrey, CR9 3WZ

EIRE readers send competition to PO Box 4546, Dublin 24.

Please tick the series you would like to receive if you are one of the lucky winners

Presents™ ❏ Enchanted™ ❏ Medical Romance™ ❏
Historical Romance™ ❏ Temptation® ❏

Are you a Reader Service™ subscriber?   Yes ❏   No ❏

Ms/Mrs/Miss/Mr ....Intials ....
(BLOCK CAPITALS PLEASE)

Surname...

Address ....

....

....Postcode............................

(I am over 18 years of age)   D8C

Closing date for entries is 31st October 1998.
One application per household. Competition open to residents of the UK and Ireland only. You may be mailed with offers from other reputable companies as a result of this application. If you would prefer not to receive such offers, please tick this box. ❏

Mills & Boon is a registered trademark of
Harlequin Mills & Boon Ltd.